My Uncle Wal the
WEREWOLF

Jackie French

illustrated by

Stephen Michael King

Angus&Robertson
An imprint

Angus&Robertson

An imprint of HarperCollins*Publishers*, Australia

First published in Australia in 2005
by HarperCollins*Publishers* Pty Limited
ABN 36 009 913 517
A member of the HarperCollins*Publishers* (Australia) Pty Limited Group
www. harpercollins.com.au

Text copyright © Jackie French 2005
Illustrations copyright © Stephen Michael King 2005

HarperCollins*Publishers*
Level 13, 201 Elizabeth Street, Sydney NSW 2000, Australia
Unit D1, 63 Apollo Drive, Rosedale Auckland 0632, New Zealand
A 53, Sector 57, Noida, UP, India
1 London Bridge Street, London, SE1 9GF, United Kingdom
2 Bloor Street East, 20th floor, Toronto, Ontario M4W 1A8, Canada
195 Broadway, New York NY 10007, USA

National Library of Australia Cataloguing-in-Publication data:

French, Jackie.
  My uncle wal the werewolf.
  ISBN 0 207 20013 0.
  1. Family – Juvenile fiction. I. King, Stephen Michael.
  II. Title (Series: French, Jackie, Wacky families; no. 5.).
A823.3

Cover and internal illustrations and design by Stephen Michael King
Typeset in Berkeley Book

To Lewis, here's another one for you.
Much love, Aunty Jacq

To the Hayes Pack
SMK

Chapter 1

Buster Rebels

It was the fattest, juiciest rat Buster had ever seen, and it was scampering across the grass in front of the Tower as though it hadn't a care in the world. The rat smelled like guts and garbage. Buster drooled. He hadn't realised he was hungry!

Snap! Buster's jaws closed round the hairy body. Crunch!

Sweet . . .

It was just as juicy as he'd thought it would be. There was nothing like a fat rat when you'd been sniffing your way across an entire mountain, decided Buster, settling down in the middle of the lawn to munch the bones. Things never seemed as bad with a rat in your belly!

'Buster? What are you doing?'

Buster gulped the last of the rat guiltily. 'Nothing, Aunty Paws!' he yelled.

'You're not spoiling your dinner, are you?' called his aunt.

'Me? No way!' yelled Buster, dropping the rat's tail and sitting on it, as Aunty Paws trotted out the Tower door.

'Where have you been?' demanded Aunty Paws worriedly. 'It's just not safe on the mountain now! You haven't been hunting for your parents, have you? You know what Uncle Wal said!'

'Me? No! Of course not,' said Buster innocently, licking a dribble of rat guts off his fur.

'Look at you!' Aunty Paws sat back on her haunches and sighed. 'You've got rat juice on your tummy. And Uncle Wal has told you a hundred times: "Change when you come home!"'

'It was just one rat,' protested Buster. 'Just one tiny little rat. Here,' he offered. He picked up the rat's tail in his mouth, stood up and offered it to Aunty Paws.

Aunty Paws gazed longingly at the rat's tail, then crunched it quickly in her strong jaws. 'You know Uncle Wal doesn't like us eating rats,' she said guiltily, swallowing the last of the tail. 'Why don't you have a nice bowl of broccoli with peanut butter? Or I could make you a porridge sandwich. They're good *human* foods!'

'I hate broccoli!' protested Buster. 'And porridge doesn't have any guts in it. Anyway, you don't like broccoli. And you haven't Changed either,' he pointed out.

Aunty Paws sighed again, her long tongue hanging out. 'We'd better both Change,' she agreed. 'Uncle Wal will be upset if he comes home and we don't look human.'

Buster felt his tail droop between his legs. Things had been so different since Mum and Dad disappeared two weeks before, and Uncle Wal took over the werewolf pack.

Dad had been the biggest, strongest werewolf on the whole of Black Mountain — except for Mum. Mum was even bigger, with golden fur and a tail like a broom.

Mum didn't mind how many rats you ate, as long as you saved some guts for her, thought Buster sadly, as he and Aunty Paws trotted back into the Tower. Dad had shown him how to snap flies out of the air, crunch the fleas that bit your tail, and find the smelliest cow pats to roll in so the deer couldn't pick up your scent.

But Mum and Dad had vanished, totally and utterly. One day they'd been there at breakfast, chewing their bones. And then they'd gone out for a run and never come back.

Buster, Uncle Flea and Aunty Paws had searched everywhere, trying to follow Mum and Dad's scent on every tree or leaf pile till Uncle Wal ordered them to leave the hunt to him. Uncle Wal was still looking for them, he told the others, every chance he got. But there'd never been the faintest sniff of Buster's parents again.

And that meant Uncle Wal was leader. And he'd *changed*.

Uncle Wal had always been good at pretending he was human. He even had a car — you had to be really good at being human to drive a car. He brought Buster human-type presents too, like balls and remote-controlled cars that went 'crunch' when you caught them.

But now Uncle Wal kept insisting that everyone else had to try to be human too, thought Buster indignantly, lifting his leg to widdle on the Tower doorpost. *Totally* human, not just some of the time!

'Buster!' growled Aunty Paws warningly.

Buster stopped mid widdle, his leg still up in the air.

'But, Aunty!' he protested. '*Someone* has to widdle on the doorpost! How will anyone know we live here, if we don't mark our doorposts?'

'Uncle Wal says we can only widdle in the bathroom!' said Aunty Paws sadly, scratching her ear with her hind paw. 'There's hardly anything to widdle on in a bathroom! And there's ...' Aunty Paws shuddered, 'a bath in there! Uncle Wal says humans never widdle on doorposts.' Aunty Paws shook her head. 'Poor things. How do they know who's been in and out if they don't leave a bit of widdle?'

'Dad used to widdle on the doorpost every day! And on the rose bushes!' protested Buster, his leg still in the air. 'Dad said werewolf rule number one is: *Learn how to produce enough widdle to cover everything in your territory every day!* Uncle Wal can go bite my bu—'

Buster froze, the last yellow drops of widdle scattering to the ground, as Uncle Wal's car zoomed up the Tower driveway. Dad had said that cars were only

good for two things — for riding in with your head out the window and your ears flying in the breeze, and for chasing. But Uncle Wal *liked* driving a car.

'Uh-oh!' Buster gazed around hurriedly. 'Hide!' he hissed to Aunty Paws. 'Before he sees that we haven't Changed!'

Buster and Aunty Paws darted behind the door as the car drew to a stop. Buster peered out, then his tail droop even further. Only Uncle Wal was in the car. So he hadn't found Mum or Dad! Every day he just kept hoping ...

Uncle Wal got out. He looked totally human in his green suit and thongs and baseball cap, thought Buster disgustedly. Uncle Wal could at least have widdled on the baseball cap, he decided, to give it a good wolf-like smell!

Uncle Wal smelled of talcum powder these days. He'd even started to use aftershave! What sort of a wolf used aftershave?

Uncle Wal looked tired. There were dark circles under his eyes. He looked around, his nostrils widening suspiciously.

'Who's been widdling on that doorpost!' snarled Uncle Wal. He bent down and sniffed again.

'Buster!' he roared, 'I can smell it was you! Come out here this minute!'

Buster slunk out from behind the door, his tail

between his legs. Uncle Wal never used to get as cross as this! 'Hello, Uncle Wal,' he muttered. 'Um, did you find any scent of Mum and Dad?' he added hopefully.

'No. And Change when I'm talking to you!' growled Uncle Wal.

Buster gritted his teeth. 'Yes, Uncle Wal,' he said obediently. He shut his eyes, nodded his head twice, then ...

Nunggg!

It was like a sneeze back to front, with a sort of tickle in between. Buster could feel his tail getting shorter, his ears getting lower, his fur disappearing and his body rising ...

And he was human.

Suddenly the world was brighter, the colours sharper, and the scents fading.

Uncle Wal stared at him. 'And get some clothes on!' he barked. 'Humans don't go naked, boy!'

Oops. Buster grabbed the doormat and held it in front of himself. At least it felt reassuringly hairy against his skin. It smelled good, too. And it covered the embarrassing bits. Changing from human to wolf was easy — you were covered in fur. But when you Changed into human form there were bald dangly bits exposed!

'That's better,' growled Uncle Wal. 'Now what do you think you're doing, eh, boy? Widdling on doorposts; prowling around in dog form!'

'I've been out on the mountain trying to track Mum and Dad! And I'm not a dog, I'm a wolf!' muttered Buster. 'Dad said widdling on posts was part of being a wolf, too! Dad was proud to be a werewolf!' he added bravely.

'What did I tell you, boy!' thundered Uncle Wal. 'You're not to go roaming around the mountain by yourself any more! It's *my* job to hunt for your parents, not yours. Are you the head of the pack now?'

'No, Uncle Wal,' muttered Buster.

'I didn't think so!' Uncle Wal's nostrils flared as he sniffed the air. 'And I smell dead rat too!'

Uncle Wal began to count on his fingers as he listed Buster's crimes. 'Not Changing for dinner, widdling on the doorpost, *and* catching rats. That's three black marks. You know what happens when you get three black marks, don't you?'

Buster looked up in alarm. 'Not ... not ...' he stammered.

'Yes!' said Uncle Wal dreadfully. 'A bath!'

Buster gulped. Not a bath! It took weeks to smell as good as he did! Dad always said make sure you *stink* was werewolf rule number two. A werewolf could tell everything from the way you smelled. A bath would wash off all that lovely dead-rat pong — and the wallaby droppings he'd rolled in — and that green bubbling ...

'Buster didn't eat the rat.' Aunty Paws stepped out from behind the door. 'I ate the rat. I felt hungry,' she lied courageously. 'I just can't get used to broccoli and peanut butter for lunch! And that spaghetti stuff may crunch when you bite the packet but it doesn't taste of anything, even if you bury it for days!'

'Silence!' barked Uncle Wal. He gazed at Buster and Aunty Paws, then shook his head. 'You're as bad as Buster! Well,' he added, 'things are going to be different around here!'

'How?' asked Buster nervously, clutching the doormat closer to his body.

'It's just not safe up here on the mountain since your parents disappeared,' declared Uncle Wal. 'We're too isolated! So I've come to a decision!'

'What?' asked Buster nervously.

'I'm putting the Tower on the market,' growled Uncle Wal.

'But you can't!' cried Aunty Paws. 'It's our home!'

'I'm sorry,' said Uncle Wal. 'But there's no choice! We're going to move into town — the whole pack of us. We're going to learn to be human! And Buster is going to school.'

School! Buster couldn't believe it. Werewolves didn't go to school! Werewolves hunted in the forest and captured their prey and howled on the cliffs at full moon. They didn't sit at desks doing maths!

'No!' yelled Buster. 'It's not fair!'

'Buster, dear, I'm sure your uncle knows best,' wavered Aunty Paws.

'He just wants us to be human because he *likes* being human!' shouted Buster. 'But I'm a wolf!'

'If you're a wolf, boy, you'll do what your pack leader orders!' snarled Uncle Wal. 'Now go get Changed, Paws! And you, boy — get some clothes on!'

Uncle Wal stomped off, into the Tower.

Chapter 2

Be a Human!

Buster let the doormat fall to the ground. 'He … he can't mean it,' he stammered.

Aunty Paws hung her head. 'He does.'

'He never used to be like this,' protested Buster desperately. 'Was he just pretending to be nice when Mum and Dad were here? We're werewolves, not humans! And I don't want to go to school!'

'It's not easy for him, suddenly being pack leader. And it doesn't matter if you want to go to school or not. The pack always does what the leader says,' said Aunty Paws quietly. 'That's what being a wolf is all about. You can obey, or you can challenge him. Or you can leave the pack.'

Aunty Paws moved closer and licked Buster's ear. 'And you're not big enough to challenge Uncle Wal yet. One day you'll be as big as your father — even bigger maybe. But now …' Aunty Paws shook her head sadly. 'We have to do what we're told.'

Buster shivered. He wished he was back in wolf form. When you were a wolf you thought mostly about what was happening now — the flea biting your bum or the great pong of a maggotty bone. But when you were human you could imagine what things *could* be like too easily.

School! Living in town, with houses around, no feral rabbits to chase, just someone's guinea pig if he was lucky!

'I'd better go and get dressed,' he muttered. He bent down and kissed Aunty Paws' furry neck, then dragged his feet upstairs to his bedroom. If he'd been in wolf form, he'd have bounded up the stairs. But he didn't dare upset Uncle Wal any further by Changing again.

Buster's room was almost at the top of the Tower, just under the battlements where Dad used to lead the pack in their monthly howl under the full moon. Afterwards they'd all slurp up the sheep guts that Uncle Flea had specially buried so they'd be all ripe and smelly ...

Buster sniffed. It hurt too much to remember the howling parties with Mum and Dad.

Where were they? How could they have possibly got lost? Mum and Dad knew every scent and every tree on the mountain! And werewolves never got lost — they just followed their scent back home again. It was impossible! But it had happened!

How could things have gone from being so good, to so bad, in just a few short weeks? thought Buster desperately.

Buster sniffed. He felt like really howling now, human-type howling with tears and sobs.

Had Mum and Dad been caught in a trap? Buster had learnt about wolf traps. But if that had happened the werewolves would have been able to smell Mum and Dad's tracks, and smell whoever had set the trap, too. Uncle Wal was the best tracker the pack had ever had. He could track a mouse across a paddock. But Uncle Wal had told them there'd been no strange smells at all on the mountain.

How could a pair of werewolves disappear without a trace?

Maybe aliens had captured them … Buster gave himself a shake. No, this was the *real* world. But what could have happened?

Buster sighed and grabbed a pair of boxers and a raincoat out of his wardrobe, and flung them on. There! He was properly dressed as a human. Uncle Wal couldn't complain now.

Buster didn't mind being human *sometimes* — after all, he was part human, as well as wolf. But he didn't want to be human all the time!

What would it be like in a human school? What if he forgot to be human and widdled on the classroom door? Or drank from the urinal, or barked in choir, or sniffed the teacher's bum? Buster bet they didn't even have corgi ice blocks at school canteens. Just human stuff like broccoli and peanut butter, or crunchy spaghetti, or raspberry jam and chips. Boring human food . . .

He couldn't be human all the time! He couldn't!

Buster flung himself on his bed. It was a round bed, big enough to turn around on six times when he was a wolf, or stretch out on when he was human.

He had to think of some way out of this. There had to be a way to stop Uncle Wal making them leave the mountain! He had to find Mum and Dad!

At least it was easier to plan in human form. Wolf form was good for hunting and tracking and speed, and learning about the world with your nose. But thoughts came more clearly when you were human.

Buster scratched a flea bite thoughtfully. If only he were a detective. He'd read a book about a detective once — Buster reckoned one of the few good things about being human was books. But he wasn't a detective. He was just an everyday type of werewolf.

Buster hesitated. He mightn't be a detective ... but he could hire one! Just like people did in books! Surely a detective could find his parents!

That was it!

Buster gulped. The only way he'd be able to find a detective was to leave the mountain and head down into town. He'd been to town before of course, but only with Uncle Wal, to do fun things like hunt through the rubbish bins and chase cars and cats and see which public toilet had the best flavoured toilet bowls. It had even been fun when Dad had taken him in wolf form too!

But to go alone ...

Buster sat up straight and scratched his ear with his hind leg, then realised he was human shaped, and bit his lip instead. If that was what it took to find Mum and Dad, he'd do it!

Tomorrow!

CHAPTER 3

Buster Sets Out

Breakfast was mashed broccoli and peanut butter as usual, and everyone was human as they ate it.

Uncle Wal glared at Uncle Flea. 'Use a spoon, man, a spoon!' he snapped.

Uncle Wal was wearing a nifty human outfit this morning — green-and-purple-striped trousers, a pink T-shirt and tie, with a fluffy woollen beanie on his head. But he looked even more tired and worried than he had the day before.

Uncle Flea stopped trying to lap his broccoli, and tried to lick his whiskers. 'Spoons, spoons, spoons,' he grumbled. 'You can't teach an old dog new tricks. What's wrong with tongues, I'd like to know?'

Uncle Wal growled softly across the table, and Uncle Flea's grumbling stopped.

Uncle Wal stood up. 'Now,' he said to Buster. 'I'm going down to town this morning to look for your parents.'

'But Mum and Dad would never leave the mountain without telling us!' protested Buster.

'Silence!' barked Uncle Wal. 'I want no puddles on the doorpost today. Understood? And no wandering about the mountain either. I could smell where you went yesterday! I'm in charge of this hunt, not you.' He glared at Buster.

'Yes, Uncle Wal,' promised Buster sincerely. After all, he planned to go to town today too, not roam the mountain!

'Everyone is to stay in human form all day. We're all going to be human from now on, so you'd better get used to it. And no fleas in the carpet!' Uncle Wal looked at Uncle Flea sternly. 'If you want to scratch, go outside. Or better still have a bath.'

'A bath!' quavered Uncle Flea. 'I've never had a bath in my life! You can't make an old dog take a bath!'

Uncle Wal showed his teeth. Uncle Wal might look human this morning, but his teeth were pure wolf. 'You'll take a bath if I say so,' he growled softly. 'Soon we're all going to have baths every day. Even,' he paused, then hissed, 'brush our teeth!'

Uncle Flea whimpered.

'I'll see you all tonight.' Uncle Wal marched out of the room, his flip-flops flapping as he went.

Buster listened to Uncle Wal's footsteps disappear down the corridor. Uncle Flea took a deep breath and began to lap his mashed broccoli and peanut butter again. Aunty Paws whined softly.

'He's so different these days!' she whispered, then shook her head sadly. 'What are you going to do today, young pup?' she asked Buster, obviously trying to change the subject.

'Oh, just sniff around,' said Buster vaguely. 'I'd better get going. See you later, everyone!'

'But Wal said we had to be human, and not roam around the mountain!' cried Aunty Paws, distressed.

Buster patted her wrinkled old hand. Aunty Paws always looked more fragile in her human form. 'I won't

let him smell me,' he assured her. 'And I'll Change back before I come home.'

'You're a good pup,' said Aunty Paws sadly. 'If only you were old enough . . .' She stopped again.

Old enough to challenge Uncle Wal, thought Buster, finishing the sentence for her. So we could keep on being wolves! Well, I'm not. But I *am* old enough to find a detective!

Buster shut his eyes, nodded his head twice, then . . .

It was like an upside-down hiccup, with a wriggle in between. Buster could feel his bum getting furrier, his ears getting more pointed, his arms getting shorter and his tail getting longer . . .

And he was a wolf.

The kitchen smelled warm and rich and meaty, and the problems of the future faded away.

Aunty Paws smiled, and picked his clothes up off the floor. 'Have fun, my puppy,' she said softly, and Buster knew that she really meant: 'Have fun as a wolf while you can.'

Buster bounced up and gave Aunty's cheek a quick lick, then gave Uncle's bum a sniff. Okay, it wasn't right to go sniffing someone when they were in human form, but it cheered Uncle Flea up. Dad always said werewolf rule number three was: *Always sniff a bloke's bum and you'll learn all there is to know about him.*

Uncle Wal's bum smells of talcum powder, thought Buster. It's as though he's stopped being a wolf altogether.

Now . . .

Buster bounded off down the corridor, his tail wagging.

CHAPTER 4

Down off Werewolf Mountain

There were so many advantages to being in wolf form, thought Buster, as he raced down the mountain and began to trot along the road between the paddocks. To begin with he was much faster — it would take him all day to walk to town if he was human!

No clothes to carry. No need for a packed lunch — he could grab a quick corgi on the way if he felt hungry; and there were always gutters, or fish ponds for a drink, or even a public toilet bowl if he felt like something sweeter.

But it was the sense of smell that was best as a werewolf, thought Buster happily, sniffing the scents of cattle droppings and old grass in the paddocks. It wasn't just that smells were richer — you could smell what happened yesterday too, and the day before, and the week before that.

Ah, yes! A calf had been born here last week … and a car had stopped here so a human kid could have a widdle. Humans! snorted Buster. They never even thought to use their widdle to mark out territory, or to tell people where they'd been. They just widdled when they needed to … mmm, yes, the kid had been carsick too, and a fox had sniffed the vomit and …

The whole world was layers and layers of smells, and as a wolf you could understand them all.

It felt good to have the wind in his ears and the feel of the dirt road under his paws. There were more cars about now. Buster wrinkled his nose — the fumes from car exhausts were so strong it was hard to smell other things when one was around. No wonder humans never used their noses, thought Buster pityingly, when they had to live with cars!

They hardly ever saw all the way up the mountain. The road was too rough and too steep to be inviting. But if any car came up, there was nothing suspicious to see — just normal-looking humans, if the werewolves were in human form, or big hairy dogs if they weren't.

And if a human caught sight of someone Changing from wolf to human — well, they'd just they were seeing things!

Buster chased each car that passed just for the fun of it, barking happily as the dust shot up from under their wheels as they overtook him.

Life was good!

Buster pulled himself up suddenly. That was the trouble with being in wolf form — you got so caught up in the joy of life, you forgot what you were doing.

A detective. That was it! He had to hire a detective to help find his parents!

Buster padded along the road, then stopped, and scratched himself thoughtfully.

Exactly how did you find a detective? Uncle Wal knew stuff like that, thought Buster. Two weeks ago he could have asked him. But two weeks ago he didn't need a detective!

A werewolf detective would just widdle on a few posts, so anyone who came along could sniff and say, 'Aha! There's been a detective here! I think I'll hire them!'

Buster shook his head. Life would be a lot simpler if humans learnt how to widdle on doorposts.

Maybe he could look in the phone book under 'detectives'. Mum had shown him how to use phone books and phones last time they'd gone into town.

But it might look odd if someone looked into a phone box and saw a dog reading the phone book. Dad said werewolf rule number four was: *Don't look different when you're down among the humans!*

Buster shook his head. He'd make sure he obeyed rule number four today, but he didn't have time to follow rule number one and widdle on all the posts. Dad would understand, he thought hopefully. Today there were even more important things to be done than widdling.

No, what he'd have to do was find an office block, Buster decided, the sort that looked like it might have a detective's office in it. Then he'd wander along the corridor, looking as much like someone's lost pet as he could, till he saw a sign like that one on the power pole that said, 'Defective'.

Buster stopped, and sat back on his haunches, and read the sign on the power pole again:

Defective for hire! All your probblems sollved! 99 Snoggle Street, corll rounnd the bacck.

Buster blinked. Surely the sign didn't really mean 'defective'. It had to be 'detective'. Maybe a 'defective' was a special kind of detective. Yes, that would be it! And Snoggle Street was only . . .

Exactly where was Snoggle Street, wondered Buster.

Well, there was only one way to find out.

Buster lifted his nose and sniffed. Rose gardens — you never *really* smelled rose gardens when you were human

— someone doing delicious bean farts two houses along, the scent of a sleeping cat and a pair of budgies, yum!... aha, he had it now! The smells of soap powder and car park and take-away chickens were only two blocks away! Just what he needed! A shopping centre!

Buster trotted along the road, ignoring the cat that stared at him from a windowsill, and the Doberman across the road. Huh! He could outbark a Doberman any day. His bum smelled twice as fierce as any Doberman's! He was a werewolf, not a yappy house dog ... Yes, there it was, the shopping centre car park. And there was a woman trudging across it, her bags of groceries in her arms.

Buster slipped underneath a four-wheel drive (hmmm, it had been in an underground car park recently, by the smell of it, and a King Charles spaniel had widdled on the back tyre two days ago). Buster waited till the woman's feet were right by his nose.

'Excuse me,' he called, 'can you tell me the way to Snoggle Street?'

'Second on the right past the garage.' The woman turned around to see who had spoken. But of course, thought Buster with glee, she never thought to look down!

'Thank you!' barked Buster quickly. He crawled out the other side of the car and raced across the car park while the woman was still looking round. No one ever looks down, thought Buster smugly. No one ever looks at a dog to see what they've got to say.

More cats ... a schnauzer. Dad would eat you for breakfast with peanut butter, you yappy bit of fur, thought Buster — some good stinky fertiliser just waiting to be rolled in ... And yes, there was the sign that said 'Snoggle Street'. Buster gazed up at the numbers on the gates — 23, 44 ...

Number 99 looked like any other house, a blob of bricks with shrubs all about it. Not even a tower to howl from, thought Buster disgustedly, and no one had bothered to widdle *anywhere* to say this place had a defective in it. There wasn't even a sign on the gate that said 'defective', or 'detective' either.

Buster peered between the shrubs. Yes, there was a sign, Buster realised. A big sign on the shed, half-hidden down the back yard: **Defective for hire. Inkyire withinn.**

Buster sat down on his haunches again. This was going to be difficult. But Dad always said that werewolf rule number five was: *If you can't sniff out a solution, use your brains instead.*

Defective
for hire
Inkyire withinn

It was time to use his brains.

Buster thought for a minute, his tongue hanging out. A cool tongue always helped him think better. Right, this was the plan ...

Buster trotted up to the shed window, then lay down in his best innocent-dog-sleeping-in-the-sun-with-his-nose-up-his-bum-just-ignore-me position. 'Excuse me?' he called.

'What is it?' A girl's head poked through the window. She peered down at Buster, ignored him, and looked around again. 'Who's there?'

'Me,' said Buster. 'There's no use looking for me,' he added quickly. 'I'm hiding behind the bushes.'

The girl's forehead wrinkled. She was about Buster's age, with the messiest ginger hair he'd ever seen, piled up like a bird's nest all around her face. Ginger freckles were scattered all over her nose and cheeks, and her eyes were the same shade of grey as the grass on Werewolf Mountain.

'Why can't I see you?' she demanded. But at least now she looked towards the

bushes, thought Buster gleefully. She
didn't even bother looking down at the
dog by the wall.

'Er ... because my business is
secret,' mumbled Buster, keeping his
nose on his paws and his mouth
half-shut while trying to look as
much like a sleeping dog as
possible. 'I'm looking for the
defective.'

'The what? Look, buster, who are you calling a
defective!' yelled the girl.

'But your sign says "defective",' argued Buster. 'How
did you know my name was Buster?' he added hopefully.
Maybe this detective-defective really was good!

The girl sighed. 'I'm not calling you Buster, I'm
calling you "buster",' she explained.

'Huh?' asked Buster.

'That's "buster" without a capital "b". It means, "You
twit; what are you talking about?" And that sign should
read detective, *not* defective. I may not be much good at
spelling,' the girl added, 'but I'm *really* good at finding
things out.'

'Excellent!' said Buster, pretending to snap sleepily
at a fly. 'Because I want to hire you to find my mum
and dad!'

'Really?' The girl's face brightened. 'That's a real case!'

Buster frowned, which did funny things to his ears. 'You mean you haven't had a real case before?'

'Of course I have,' said the girl hurriedly. 'I'm a detective, aren't I?' She grabbed a pen and what looked like a used Christmas card from somewhere inside, and turned it over to the blank side. 'Now, when did you last see your parents?'

'Two weeks ago! They went for a run and didn't come back.'

The girl scribbled on the back of the Christmas card. 'And what do the police say?'

'Er . . . we haven't been to the police . . .'

The girl looked up. 'Why not?' she demanded.

'We ... er ... we just didn't,' said Buster helplessly. How could he and Aunty Paws and Uncle Flea tell the police to look for two werewolves who could be in human form?

'But you looked for them?'

'Yes, me and Aunty Paws and Uncle Flea sniffed everywhere, but we couldn't smell ...' Buster broke off.

'Sniffed!' exclaimed the girl. 'You *sniffed* for them?'

'I mean looked,' said Buster quickly. 'We looked everywhere!'

The girl was looking at him strangely. 'You're a dog!' she declared suddenly. 'A talking dog!'

Chapter 5

A Red-haired Detective

Buster looked up at her. 'I'm not a talking dog!'

The girl snorted. 'Oh yeah? You've got paws, a hairy nose, and you're talking. Conclusion: you're a talking woof woof. You don't even have to be a detective to work that one out. Hey, are you a mutant dog? Or genetically modified?'

'I'm not a dog at all!' Buster gulped. Dad always said werewolf rule number six was: *Don't tell anyone you're a werewolf.* Humans were terrified of werewolves, Dad said. The one sure way to get a human to widdle was to let them see your fangs, and they'd let it all go in terror.

But this was different.

'I'm a werewolf,' Buster confessed. He waited for the girl to shriek, or maybe faint in a puddle on the floor. But all she said was, 'Yeah, right. And I'm Winkums the elf who lives in the washing machine.'

Buster blinked. 'Are you really?' he demanded.

The girl sighed again. 'Just my luck to get a client from the planet dumb dumb. No, I am not a cute little elf. And you don't look like a werewolf either.'

'But I am!' insisted Buster.

'Sure you are. Oh, what big fangs you have,' said the girl coolly.

'My fangs will get bigger when I'm older!' yelled Buster.

'And I suppose it's a full moon up there and when it's gone you'll be a human ...'

'I can turn into a human anytime I want to!' shouted Buster.

'Well, go on then. Do it!' ordered the girl.

'Alright. I will!'

Buster grinned, his long tongue lolling out of his mouth. He'd show her!

Buster shut his eyes, nodded his head twice, then ...

It was like a burp that went backwards, with a rumble in between. He could feel his head getting higher, his arms getting longer, his body getting barer ...

And he was human.

The world was full of colours again, and different shapes, some bits clear and others indistinct. He'd never realised the girl's eyes were quite so green, not grey at all!

The girl stared at him. She looked him up and down ... and down, then quickly looked back up again. And then she blushed.

'Turn back at once!' she ordered.

'But you said . . .' began Buster.

'Look, buster,' said the girl, 'in case you haven't noticed, you're naked! Nude! Undressed! Bare-bummed! I'm not going anywhere with a kid who has his you-know-what hanging out. Understood? And I don't have any spare clothes for you, before you ask.

Mum might come down here any minute, and if she sees a naked boy near my shed she's going to have kittens! And no, she's not a were-cat, she's an average sort of mum who does not expect to see naked boys in her back yard! So get that fur back on. Now!'

Buster shut his eyes, nodded his head twice, then ...

It was like a fart that tried to somersault, with a sort of prickle in between. He could feel his hands getting smaller, his tongue getting longer, and the bits that the girl objected to getting smaller too, and neatly covered in fur.

And he was back to being a wolf. Once again the world turned into rich smells, and the feeling that any problem could be solved as long as you could bite it.

The girl let out a long breath.

'Wow,' she said. 'You really are ...' She stopped. 'You know, I think we need to start again.'

Chapter 6

Detective Prunella

'Right,' said the girl, 'my name's Prunella and I'm a detective. Well, I am in the school holidays anyway.'

'Prunella!' chortled Buster. 'You mean like prunes and custard, prunes that give you the runs, prunes that ...'

Prunella glared at him. 'You're a talking dog called Buster and you think *my* name is funny!'

'Well it is,' observed Buster. 'And I'm not a dog. I told you, I'm a werewolf!'

'Look, buster,' said Prunella. This time Buster was pretty sure her 'buster' still didn't start with a capital 'b'. 'Do you want this case solved or not?'

'Yes,' said Buster meekly.

'Then no wisecracks about my name.' The girl looked around. 'Maybe you'd better come inside. A talking dog is better than a naked boy, but if Mum sees me yakking to a dog, she'll think I've gone bonkers.'

It was hot inside the shed. Buster sat on the faded mat with his tongue hanging out.

'You don't have a saucer of water, do you?' he panted. It was alright for her, in shorts and a T-shirt. He had a thick fur coat on!

'Can you drink out of this?' Prunella held up a chipped, old mug that was full of pens.

'Sure,' said Buster.

He gazed around the shed while Prunella tipped the pens out onto the desk and filled up the mug from the tap in the garden. This shed was the messiest place he'd ever seen! It smelled good too, of mice and rotting paper.

There were bookshelves everywhere, crammed with books with titles like *The Amazing Bonzo and the Case of the Disappearing Emeralds*. That book looked cool, thought Buster.

There was a desk with only three legs — the fourth side was held up by a pile of books.

On top of the desk was a computer so old, it could have been steam-powered. There was a stack of old birthday cards, turned blank-side up, a chair, and an armchair with a sagging seat. Someone had shoved a lawn mower in the corner, as well as a spade, an empty bird cage and the back-half of a bicycle. That delicious smell of mouse droppings was all around.

Buster wondered if Prunella would mind if he tried to catch the mouse. He could do with a snack. Better not, he decided. Dad always said that humans were strange that way. As soon as food began to wriggle they'd scream.

Not that Prunella looked like a screamer, but still . . .

Prunella came back inside and put the mug on the concrete floor. Buster lapped the water gratefully. It didn't taste of much; no leaves or wallaby droppings — just a faint taste of chemicals. But he was thirsty.

'Thanks', he said, then jumped up on the armchair, turned around three times, and collapsed onto the sagging seat.

'You'd better not let Mum see you on that seat,' Prunella warned. 'She doesn't allow dogs on the furniture.'

'But I'm not a dog!' began Buster. 'I'm a . . .'

'Yeah, I know, I know. You're a werewolf. You try explaining that to my mum,' said Prunella. 'Anyhow, I bet she'd say no werewolves on the furniture either. Now, let's get down to business.'

She picked up a card that said 'To a good girl on her birthday, love Grandma', and began to take notes on the blank side. 'You said your mum and dad disappeared?'

'Exactly how many cases have you had?' inquired Buster suddenly.

Prunella glared at him. 'Enough.' she said. 'Now, let's start at the beginning . . .

Half an hour later the card was full, and so was the back of 'Merry Christmas from Uncle Peter' and 'What will the Easter Bunny bring you this year?' Prunella gazed at her notes thoughtfully, while Buster hunted a flea that was biting his tummy.

'So you see,' Buster concluded, 'it's all just impossible! Mum and Dad just vanished, leaving no scent at all, and that simply can't happen. Unless they were captured by aliens, of course.'

'Or went in a car,' suggested Prunella.

'But . . . but cars hardly ever come up the mountain. Except for Uncle Wal's,' he added. 'Uncle Wal's a really good driver,' he added proudly. Uncle Wal might growl a lot lately, but he was pack leader. And until Mum and Dad vanished he'd been really nice.

'How do you all make a living then?' asked Prunella curiously.

'We sell sheepskins and rabbit fur and ...'

'How do you get the ... actually, no don't tell me,' said Prunella hurriedly. 'Look, if there's a road, your parents might have left in a car.'

Buster blinked. 'Why would Mum and Dad want to go in a car?'

'That's what we've got to find out! So the first thing we have to do now is ...' Prunella stopped. 'Would you mind not doing that?' she demanded.

'Doing what?'

'Licking your you-know-whats!'

'Oh, sorry,' said Buster guiltily, putting his hind leg down. Dad had always said that werewolf rule number seven was: *Don't lick your you-know-whats when you're in human form.* Buster supposed that also meant, *don't lick your you-know-whats when a human knows you're a werewolf.*

'As I was saying,' continued Prunella sharply. 'The first thing to do is to call all the hospitals in the area just in case they had an accident.'

'But what if Mum and Dad were in wolf form?'

'And we'll call all the dog pounds and vets, and maybe the police too, in case someone has reported seeing wolves around. What do your mum and dad look like?'

'Well, Dad is dark and hairy.'

'When he's human, I mean,' said Prunella.

'When he's human too. And Mum has golden fur and a really bushy tail and when she's human, she's blonde and her tail disappears. And they'll both be ...' Buster stopped.

'Well?' demanded Prunella.

'If they're in human form they'll be naked,' whispered Buster, 'because they didn't take any clothes with them.'

'Great,' sighed Prunella. 'We're hunting two naked people, or two wolves who talk. Alright, I'll ring around and see if any naked people have been taken to hospital, and you ring the vets and places like that. That is, if you know how to use a phone.'

'Of course I know how to use a phone,' said Buster affronted. 'I've used one lots of times.'

'Lots?' demanded Prunella.

'Well, once,' admitted Buster. 'Mum showed me! But I know how it's done!'

'Good. Then we'll use the phones in the house. Mum's an architect so we've got two phone lines — one for her work and one for us.'

'But what will your mum say if she finds me in your house?' demanded Buster.

'She'll say "What a cute little doggie," then go back to her work,' said Prunella. 'Mum's not really interested in what I do,' she added a bit sadly. 'She thinks being a detective is silly.'

'But I'm not a cute little doggie. I'm a werewolf!' protested Buster.

Prunella snorted. 'You try telling that to my mum! On second thoughts, don't!'

CHAPTER 7

The Search Begins

Prunella's house smelled of ice cream, and detergent, and the bacon and eggs they'd had for breakfast. Buster's mouth watered. Bacon and eggs weren't as delicious as a nice smelly rat, or a bowl of fox terrier guts, but they were better than mashed broccoli and peanut butter.

Buster trod carefully over the polished kitchen floor. He hoped his claws wouldn't slip.

'In here,' said Prunella, opening a door. 'This is the family room.'

Buster sniffed it. There was no smell of mouse in here, or bacon and eggs either. Just more polish and the sort of fluffy carpet that no one had ever accidentally done *that* on, and two big sofas that looked to be the sort that you weren't allowed to sit on, or you might leave fur on them, not to mention fleas.

'What if your mum comes in?' he asked.

'She won't,' said Prunella shortly. 'She'll be in her study working. Mum doesn't care what I do, as long as

43

'I'm quiet about it and don't make a mess. Mum hates mess. And I'm messy all the time,' she added.

'What about your dad?' asked Buster. He could smell a small lost space inside her when Prunella had talked about her mum.

'He lives overseas,' said Prunella, even more shortly. 'He sends me Christmas presents when he remembers.'

'Oh,' said Buster. He couldn't think of what else to say. He might have lost his parents, but at least they'd loved him. And his uncles and aunt all loved him too. Even Uncle Wal used to throw empty ice-cream cartons for him to snap out of the air and play human games like bury the football in the garden so no one can find it. Prunella smelled so sad when she talked about her mum!

Prunella interrupted his thoughts. 'You use that phone, I'll use the one over here,' she said.

'Um,' said Buster.

Prunella sighed impatiently. 'What?' she demanded.

'I can't use a phone with paws!' Buster pointed out. 'I'll have to Change back into a human. And if I Change back into a human I won't have any clothes on again.'

'I didn't think of that.' Prunella was blushing, Buster realised. 'Um, how about I get you a towel so you can, um, cover yourself up?'

'Good idea,' said Buster.

Prunella was back a few seconds later. She handed

Buster a big towel that smelled strongly of washing powder and sunlight.

'Turn your back,' said Buster.

'Don't worry,' declared Prunella. 'I don't want to see *anything* till you've got that towel wrapped round you!'

Buster shut his eyes, nodded his head twice, then ...

It was like an upside-down wriggle, with a sort of bump, bump, bump in between. He could feel his paws getting longer, his body getting shorter, and his tail vanishing somewhere up his backbone ...

And he was a boy again.

The world lost nearly all its smell and most of its simplicity. Suddenly worry gripped him more and more, and all the possibilities crowded in, as well. What if Mum and Dad were hurt? What if they'd lost their memory?

Buster gulped. Prunella had to find them, he thought as he wrapped the towel around his waist. She had to!

Phoning was hard work. There seemed to be a million hospitals in the city, and police stations and dog pounds. Half the time there wasn't even a person on the other end, just a computer voice that said, 'press one if you want ... and two if you want ...' and then gave a list that didn't mention lost werewolves at all.

Finally Prunella put the phone down. 'No one has heard of them,' she said wearily. 'Do you think ...' She broke off and stared at Buster. 'What's wrong?'

'Someone's coming!'

'It'll be Mum! Quick, hide!'

'There's no time!' Buster shut his eyes, nodded his head twice, then ...

It was like a case of hiccups that started in his toes, with a sort of fidget on the way. He could feel his jaw getting shorter, his eyes getting further apart, and the towel dropping off as his body got lower and lower . . .

And he was a wolf again.

The world smelled sharp and much too clean. 'Off the sofa!' hissed Prunella. Buster jumped onto the floor just as someone opened the door.

Prunella's mum smelled of soap and hand cream and computers. Buster couldn't smell computers when he was human shaped, but as a wolf he could smell every chip and wire.

'Prunella, darling?' Prunella's mum stepped into the room. 'I thought I heard voices. Oh! What a cute little dog!'

'Woof,' said Buster, sitting on his haunches and letting his tongue hang out. He cocked his head to look as cute as possible. 'Woof, woof wooffie, woof.'

'I was ... er ... trying out different voices,' said Prunella hurriedly. 'In case I want to disguise myself for my detective business.'

Her mum blinked. 'Your detective business. Oh yes, that. Darling, wouldn't you rather, well, I don't know, have ballet lessons? Or go horse riding over the holidays? All girls like horses, don't they?'

Prunella's jaw set. 'I like being a detective.'

'Yes, but …' her mum sighed. She looked down at Buster again. 'Darling, I know he's a cute little dog, but I did say we couldn't have one. Dogs are so messy and you know I'm allergic to dog hair.'

'Woof, woof,' said Buster, trying to look like a dog who'd never even thought of scratching his fur or sitting on the sofa.

'It's okay, Mum,' said Prunella 'He's just … er … visiting.'

'Oh, you mean he's a friend's dog and you're looking after him?'

'Just for the day,' said Prunella. 'In fact, just for the morning. It's time I took him back now. Come on, Buster, walkies!'

'Woof, woof, woof,' said Buster sourly. It was bad enough to have to pretend to be a dog, not a wolf. But she didn't have to talk baby talk to him!

'Oh good.' Buster could hear the relief in her mum's voice.

'And he hasn't brushed any dog hair on the sofa,' added Prunella bitterly.

'Are you sure?'

'Quite sure,' said Prunella. 'Here, boy!' She whistled at Buster and clicked her fingers.

Buster leapt up off the floor and trotted up to her. He felt like biting her ankle, but decided against it. He needed her more than she needed him.

'Woof, woof,' he muttered, and followed Prunella out the door.

As soon as they were in the garden he looked around. No one was looking. 'What were you playing at!' he exploded. 'What do you think I am? A shih-tzu?'

Prunella glared at him. 'There's no need to swear!'

'I'm not swearing! A shih-tzu is a dog! And even if I was swearing you deserved it!'

'What do you mean?'

'All that "here boy!" stuff! And whistling! Whistling!' repeated Buster furiously.

'Well, you were supposed to be pretending to be a dog!' said Prunella indignantly. 'It's normal to whistle at dogs.'

'I'm not a dog. I'm a werewolf! We're ferocious!' Buster added angrily. 'You know — fangs, dripping teeth.'

'Well, shih-tzu to you, too! What was I supposed to say!' demanded Prunella, fuming. 'This is a ferocious werewolf, Mum. He's my new client.'

'No. Of course not! But *nobody* — *nobody* — *whistles at werewolves!* It's werewolf rule number eight!'

'Well, wacky-doo,' said Prunella. 'Look, buster,' and Buster knew that it was 'buster' with a small 'b' again. 'Let me tell you rule number one to being a detective. If you're in disguise you *stay* in disguise. You were disguised as a dog. A "trying to look cute" little puppy dog. So I whistled.'

Buster cocked his head to one side and thought about it. It sounded alright, though he'd rather be in human form to think about it. It was easier to think about things when you were human.

'Well, okay,' he said reluctantly. He sat down to scratch an itch on his left shoulder, then said, 'What do we do now?'

'There's only one thing we can do,' said Prunella. 'We have to go back to the scene of the crime!'

Chapter 8

Bum Sniffing

'What crime?' asked Buster.

Prunella sighed. 'Look, your mum and dad wouldn't have just left you. And they don't sound dumb enough to get lost. And they didn't have an accident either, because we've checked all the hospitals, vets and pounds. So that just leaves one thing!'

Buster tried to follow that thought with his wolf brain. 'What?'

'They must have been kidnapped.'

'But they're werewolves!'

'Okay, wolfnapped! Honestly,' exclaimed Prunella, 'I'd have thought you'd have worked it out for yourself.'

Buster shook his head. 'It never even occurred to me,' he said, 'or to Uncle Flea or Aunty Paws either. Kidnapping, I mean wolfnapping just isn't part of a wolf's world.'

'But what about when you're human?'

'None of us are human much. Or we weren't,' he added bitterly. 'Except for Uncle Wal.'

'Then why didn't Uncle Wal think of it? You said he drives a car! He must have wondered if your mum and dad vanished in a car.'

Buster tried to work it out. 'Maybe. Maybe he was too busy being leader of the pack. It's a big responsibility, being pack leader,' he added.

'Hmmm. I suppose.' Prunella didn't seem very convinced. 'Well, come on, we'd better walk down to the shops. There's a taxi rank there.'

Buster blinked. 'Why?'

Prunella sighed. 'So we can go to Werewolf Mountain — the scene of the crime — of course.'

'Why can't we phone for a cab?'

'Duh,' said Prunella. 'Mum would want to know why we needed a cab. She'd offer to drive us. Mum may not think much of what I do, but she does the dutiful Mum thing.'

'Um.' Buster wondered whether to say anything, but there had been such hollowness in Prunella's voice. 'She does love you, you know.'

'Who? Mum? She thinks I'm a mess,' said Prunella.

Buster tried to find the words. 'She just thinks you're ... different ... from her. But she does love you. She thinks a lot of you, too. She just doesn't know how to say it.'

'How do you know?' asked Prunella suspiciously.

'I sniffed her bum, of course,' said Buster.

'You did what!' roared Prunella.

'I sniffed her bum,' said Buster matter-of-factly. 'When I was sitting on my haunches next to her. You can learn a lot about a person by sniffing their bum.'

'You sniffed my mum's bum! My mum's actual bum? How dare you!' yelled Prunella.

Buster blinked. 'I couldn't help it,' he added. 'It's a wolf thing. If you're near a bum, you sniff it. I didn't get too close,' he added. 'Not a right-up-into-the-bum-hole sort of sniff. Just a, well, you know, an everyday hello-what-are-you-thinking-about, and what-did-you-have-for-breakfast? sort of sniff.'

'No, I don't know!' Prunella glared at him. A thought suddenly struck her. 'You haven't been sniffing my bum, have you?' she demanded, even more suspiciously.

'I ... er ...' stammered Buster. How was he going to

get out of this one?

'You have! You've sniffed my bum! How dare you!' shrieked Prunella.

'Prunella, darling? Is anything wrong?' Prunella's mum leaned out the window.

Prunella lowered her voice. 'What? Wrong? No, why should anything be wrong?'

'You were yelling,' her mum pointed out.

'Er ... it was at the dog.' Prunella glared at Buster. 'He was about to lift his leg on the front door — he's not toilet-trained. So I yelled at him.'

Her mum sighed. 'Sounds like the sooner you take him back the better.'

'Exactly,' said Prunella, glaring at Buster. 'I bet he's

got fleas, too. And probably mange.'

Buster stopped scratching. 'Woof,' he muttered indignantly. What was wrong with having a few fleas? It was sort of friendly, having fleas. And you always had something to scratch if you were bored.

'Well, I'm glad he's going. See you at dinner, darling.'

'Yes, Mum,' said Prunella. She hesitated. 'Mum . . .'

'Yes?' asked her mum.

'I love you,' muttered Prunella.

Her mum looked startled, then very, very pleased. 'I love you too, darling,' she said, 'very much indeed. Should we have pizza for dinner?'

'Definitely,' said Prunella. 'I love pizza,' she added, as her mum's head vanished again. 'You get to eat it with your fingers.'

'Me too,' said Buster without thinking. 'Mouse pizza especially. Aunty Paws makes great mouse pizza. She spreads the mouse guts all over the tomato sauce, then covers it all with cheese.' Suddenly he remembered he was angry with her. '*Who* isn't house-trained?' he barked.

'You,' said Prunella calmly, beginning to walk down the road.

'I am so too!' flared Buster, trotting at her heels in a huff. 'I've been house-trained since I was a puppy.' Dad had always said that was werewolf rule number nine: *Never do 'that' on the carpet.* And he hadn't!

'You're not house-trained. You sniffed my mum's bum. And my bum,' she added. 'In my book, being house-trained means *no bum sniffing*.'

Buster said nothing. He trotted after her for a while,

trying to work her out. She didn't *smell* angry. She smelled ... what was it? Happy about her mum, in spite of the way he'd found out about it. And eager to find out what had happened to his parents too. And ... and ... and she was wondering ...

Suddenly he understood. 'Your bum smells really nice,' he added. 'Sort of ... friendly.'

Prunella stopped. 'Friendly?'

'Yes. And ... and detective-like.'

'Detective-like,' said Prunella slowly. Suddenly she grinned. 'I like that. I smell like a detective. You must have a really great nose,' she added.

'The best,' said Buster modestly. 'It runs in the family. My dad can sniff out wallaby droppings from half a kilometre away. And my mum can smell what someone is thinking even before they've thought it.'

'It must be great to be able to smell what people are thinking,' said Prunella enviously. 'It'd be a great help as

a detective.'

'It's the best way to understand the world,' agreed Buster. 'The trouble is . . .'

'What?' asked Prunella.

'When you're in wolf form you just don't understand things so well. You can smell in wolf form, but you have to be in human form to really think about it. It's like you can't do both at once.

'But when you're with me, *you* can smell and I can think,' said Prunella triumphantly. She grinned at him.

Buster grinned back, his tongue hanging out of the side of his mouth. 'Sounds good to me! And we've got a sixth sense,' he added proudly.

'What's that?' demanded Prunella.

'Don't know,' admitted Buster. 'Wolves just *know* things sometimes. But I don't know how it works.'

'Cool!' said Prunella. 'Okay, Buster, you use your nose sense and your sixth sense, and I'll use the other four! Now let's get going!'

Chapter 9

Back to Werewolf Mountain

'No dogs,' said the taxi driver flatly, glancing at Buster from over his newspaper.

'But he's a really well-behaved dog!' pleaded Prunella. Buster sat back on his haunches and tried to look cute. 'Woof, woof, woof,' he yapped, as sweetly as he could.

'He won't chew the seat, I promise. He won't even get hair on it. He'll just sit on the floor at my feet!'

Buster glared at her. Him! Sit on the floor! The only way to ride in a car was with your head out the window and your tongue lolling out and your ears flapping in the wind!

But it didn't matter. 'No dogs,' said the taxi driver again. He didn't even look up this time.

'Well shih-tzu, mate,' muttered Buster, lifting his leg on the back tyre then following Prunella behind a line of giant rubbish bins. 'I told you he wouldn't take dogs,' he added. 'We'll have to run up the mountain instead.'

'No way,' said Prunella. 'It's what, six kilometres! You may have four legs, buster, but I've only got two. Nope, you'll just have to Change back.'

'But if I Change I'll be, you know, naked,' protested Buster.

Prunella thought for a moment, then peered into the nearest garbage bin and hauled out half a dozen plastic bags. She emptied the rubbish out of them, and began tying them together.

Buster sniffed the garbage. Aha! An ancient hamburger, three disposable nappies filled with baby poo, six half-rotten oranges. Yum! 'Like a bit?' he asked, offering Prunella a green bit of bun and soggy meat.

Prunella snorted, her hands still full of plastic bags. Buster began to chew the hamburger, then a thought came to him. 'What are you doing with those plastic bags?' he demanded.

'Making you some clothes.'

'Out of plastic bags! They've had yuck in them!'

'You're the one who's got his nose in baby poo,' said Prunella calmly.

'I'm eating the hamburger, not the nappies!' protested Buster. 'And yuck is fine when I'm a wolf. You expect me to be a human in that ... thing.' He gazed at it suspiciously.

'It's a plastic swimming costume,' said Prunella. 'See? It goes round here ... and here ... then you tie it here. And you don't have to wear it long. Just while we're in the taxi.'

'Well, I ... um ...' Buster swallowed the last bit of mouldy hamburger. If this was what it took to find Mum and Dad, he supposed he could stand it. He glanced around, but he couldn't see anyone looking ...

Buster shut his eyes, nodded his head twice, then ...

61

It was like a tummy ache that felt good, not bad, with a sort of giggle on the way. He could feel his teeth getting smaller, his tongue getting shorter, and bum smells getting definitely less interesting . . .

And he was a boy again.

The world was brighter and . . .

'Aaark! Magic! Help help!'

Buster gazed round frantically.

'You nincompoop!' hissed Prunella. 'Why didn't you check that no one was looking before you Changed!'

'I did check! But I couldn't see over the rubbish bin. It's your fault! You should have warned me.'

'My fault?' began Prunella. 'It's your . . .'

The elderly woman was clasping her heart. 'That dog! It . . . it turned into a boy! Help! Help!'

Prunella galloped over and grabbed the woman's shopping before it fell out of her hands. 'No, really,' she soothed. 'I was looking all the time. It must just have been a trick of the light. See, he's just a normal kid!'

The woman stopped screaming for a second, and stared at Buster. Then she began to scream again. 'Help, help!' she shrieked. 'A naked boy! There's a naked boy in the car park!'

Prunella dashed back to Buster. 'Quick,' she hissed, 'get your swimming costume on.'

Buster began to struggle into the clammy plastic.

'Stupid woman,' he muttered. 'Can't she tell the difference between a dog and a werewolf!'

People were staring at them now. Another woman came over to the screaming lady and put her arm around her comfortingly. 'What's going on?' she demanded.

'Sorry! I have to get my brother to the swimming pool! It's time for his big race!' cried Prunella. 'Hurry!' she hissed to Buster as she grabbed his hand, dragged him over to the taxi and opened the door.

The taxi driver put down his newspaper. 'No dogs ...' he began.

'I don't have a dog!' snapped Prunella. 'This is my brother and he has to get to his big swimming race. We'll give you double fare if you get him there on time.'

The taxi driver glanced down at Buster's plastic swimming togs, glanced out the window at the gathering crowd, then shrugged. 'Okay. Double fare. Where to?'

'Werewolf Mountain,' said Buster, for once in his life trying to shut out what his nose was telling him. Now he was a human, those bags smelled yuck.

'There's no swimming pool on Werewolf Mountain!' protested the driver.

'Yes there is,' said Prunella hurriedly. 'It's just been built. Hurry!'

The taxi screeched away from the curb. Buster gave a sigh of relief. 'Can I take these off now?' he whispered.

'Only if you want to get thrown out of the cab for being naked,' snapped Prunella. 'What are you doing?'

'Winding down the window.' Buster thrust his head out the window. His ears were the wrong shape for flying in the wind, but it still felt good.

'What do you think you're doing!' yelled the driver.

The taxi slowed down again. 'I'm not taking you kids anywhere if you play the fool like that!'

'Triple fare!' cried Prunella desperately. She nudged Buster. 'Look, buster, get your head in, you dill pickle.'

Buster pulled his head in reluctantly. Some people had no sense of fun.

But it was fascinating looking at the streets he'd run through as a wolf. Things looked so different when you were human! The flowers had colours, instead of scents. The houses had shapes that you never noticed when you were more interested in cats, dogs and guinea pigs and the delicious garden additives like blood and bone and chicken poo.

But now he was worried too about his missing parents. Wolves lived in the present. But now he was a boy again, his parents' loss ate at him like acid.

Could Prunella really find them? Maybe, he thought hopefully. She'd been pretty good with the phone calls, and handling her mum and the taxi driver . . .

The landscape outside changed. Houses gave way to paddocks; paddocks gave way to scattered trees; the trees gave way to bush. The taxi began to climb the mountain.

The scenery changed again. The bush was lusher here. Fat-stemmed creepers hung from the trees, and giant boulders, half the size of houses, seemed to grow out of the hillside.

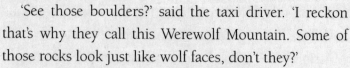

'See those boulders?' said the taxi driver. 'I reckon that's why they call this Werewolf Mountain. Some of those rocks look just like wolf faces, don't they?'

Prunella coughed. 'You could be right,' she said.

Buster looked at the rocks longingly. When he'd been a little puppy, Dad and Uncle Wal used to take him scrambling up the boulders. He and Dad would howl at the moon while Uncle Wal played the same tune on his guitar.

'Hey, stop dreaming!' Prunella nudged him. 'Where are we going?'

Buster thrust the memories away.

'Right here!' he whispered urgently. 'This is where Mum and Dad's scent finished.'

'Stop the cab!' cried Prunella to the driver.

The taxi lurched to a halt. The driver looked around. 'Where's the swimming pool?' he demanded.

'It's a new design,' said Prunella hurriedly. 'It doesn't use any water. Better exercise that way. How much do we owe you?'

The driver calculated. 'Thirty dollars and seventy-seven cents,' he said.

'Fine.' Prunella opened the cab door. 'Pay the driver,' she added to Buster.

'What?' Buster stared. 'How?'

'With money. You know,' Prunella spoke slowly as though to an idiot, 'm-o-n-e-y.'

'But I don't have any! How would I carry any money dressed like this!' Or as a wolf either, he thought, but he didn't say that aloud in case the taxi driver heard.

'But you're my client,' protested Prunella. 'Clients always pay expenses.'

'How can I . . .' began Buster.

The taxi driver sighed. 'Look, kids, are you going to pay me or not? Because if you aren't . . .' He left the threat unsaid.

'We'll pay,' said Buster hurriedly. 'Just keep driving another kilometre up the road.' Uncle Flea or Aunty Paws would pay for the taxi.

But that would mean taking Prunella back to the Tower. Buster could hear Dad's voice in his head. Werewolf rule number ten: *Never take a human back to your den!*

But there was no way out.

CHAPTER 10

Back to the Tower

The taxi driver stared out at the Tower as the taxi drew up to the gate. 'What *is* this place?' he whistled, gazing at the high stone walls, the narrow windows and the flat-topped roof.

'Home,' said Buster shortly, as Aunty Paws trotted out the door to see what the noise was. She sat on her haunches and cocked her head at the car, then loped back into the house.

'Fine-looking dog, that,' said the taxi driver. 'Irish wolfhound, isn't it? And that's a grand one too,' he added, as Uncle Flea galloped round the corner and skidded to a stop.

'Groowwl, woof!' snarled Uncle Flea.

'It's only me!' yelled Buster. He hurriedly got out of the taxi, frantically grabbing his plastic-bag swimming togs so they didn't slip.

Uncle Flea subsided.

'Wonderful training,' said the taxi driver admiringly. 'You'd think that dog understood every word you said!'

'Woof,' said Uncle Flea warningly, casting the taxi driver a look that said he was dreaming of taxi-driver steaks.

'I'll just tell Aunty we're here,' began Buster, when Aunty Paws trotted out of the house again.

But this time she was human. Buster watched as Prunella and the taxi driver stared at her. What were they looking at? he wondered. Aunty Paws had remembered to get dressed! She'd even brought her handbag!

'I owe the driver thirty dollars and seventy-seven cents,' he told her hurriedly. 'I'm sorry, Aunty Paws.'

'It doesn't matter, Buster,' said Aunty Paws gently. She counted out the money into the driver's hand as Prunella got out of the taxi.

Aunty Paws glanced at Prunella uncertainly. 'And this is . . .'

'This is Prunella, Aunty Paws,' said Buster. The taxi roared away in a stink of exhaust with Uncle Flea barking happily, as he chased it down the road. 'She's . . . um, she's human!' he confessed. 'Prunella, this is my Aunty Paws.'

'Pleased to meet you, Mrs ...' said Prunella. She was still trying not to stare.

'Just call me Aunty Paws,' Aunty Paws said kindly.

'Prunella is a detective,' explained Buster. 'She's helping me find Mum and Dad. And she *knows* about us,' he added.

Aunty Paws stared in alarm. 'But, Buster, a *human* ...' she began.

'Aunty, we *have* to find Mum and Dad,' Buster burst out. 'They can't have just vanished! And Prunella can help us!'

'But your Uncle Wal is looking for your parents,' said Aunty Paws uncertainly.

'I think,' said Prunella slowly, 'we'd better have a chat about Buster's Uncle Wal.'

Buster stared at her. So did Aunty Paws. 'Why?' Buster demanded.

Aunty Paws laid a hand on his arm. 'Let's wait till we're inside, eh? And lunch — I'm sure you can both do with some lunch.'

Buster nodded enthusiastically. The mouldy bit of hamburger seemed hours away. And Prunella hadn't even eaten any of it. Buster wondered suddenly if maybe he shouldn't have offered her some of the garbage. He sighed. It was so difficult to know what good manners were, with a human.

He and Prunella followed Aunty Paws inside. Prunella gazed around, her eyes wide. 'It's ... just so different!' she breathed.

'How?' demanded Buster.

'Well, the ceiling's really low!'

'Wolves like to feel secure,' explained Aunty Paws.

'And all the doggie doors.'

'Can't be bothered with the hand and doorknob thing,' said Aunty Paws.

'And the giant sofas.'

'Nothing like all of us snuggled up on the sofa together,' said Buster.

'And the ... the smell ...'

Aunty Paws beamed. 'It's lovely, isn't it? You can tell the whole history of our pack by that smell.'

'Um, yes,' said Prunella faintly.

Uncle Flea bounded past them, still in his wolf shape. He growled at Prunella, then bounded up and licked Buster's face. 'What have you got those plastic bags around your bum for?' he demanded, giving Buster's cheek one last wet swipe.

'Oh, these?' Buster stripped them off, then stopped as Prunella quickly shut her eyes. 'Oh, I forgot.'

Buster shut his eyes, nodded his head twice, then ...

Nunggg!

It was like a bounce that went inside out, with a shiver on the way. He could feel his tongue getting wetter, his nose getting drier, and the safe warmth of fur all over him, specially the bits that might embarrass Prunella ...

And he was a wolf again.

The world was simpler and smellier and hopefully had a ball for him to catch somewhere soon ...

Buster pulled his mind back to the matter at hand.

'You see ...' he began, then added hurriedly, 'no, Uncle Flea. No! Down!'

Uncle Flea looked round inquiringly. 'What's wrong?'

'Prunella doesn't like her bum being sniffed!' said Buster desperately. 'I'm sorry,' he added to Prunella, 'Uncle Flea doesn't meet many humans. He doesn't turn human much either.'

'Always feel too high when I'm up on two legs,' said Uncle Flea frankly. 'Can't get used to a nose that doesn't work either.'

'Me too,' agreed Aunty Flea. 'I've never really got the hang of being human.'

'Then that's why you're ...' Prunella halted.

'Why what?' demanded Buster.

'Um, nothing.' Prunella bit her lip.

Uncle Flea sniffed. 'Doesn't smell like nothing,' he observed. 'Smells like ... something about you, Paws. Something she thinks is funny.'

'No, not funny,' said Prunella hurriedly. 'Aunty Paws just looks ... different ... that's all.'

'What sort of different?' insisted Buster.

'Just the way she's dressed,' said Prunella awkwardly.

Aunty Paws blinked. 'What's wrong with wearing shorts and a ballet skirt and a tracksuit top?'

'Nothing,' Prunella assured her. 'Just ... maybe not all together!'

'But they fit!' objected Aunty Paws. 'And they cover up all the bits!'

'There's a bit more to clothes than that,' said Prunella tactfully.

'Humans,' sighed Aunty Paws. 'No offence,' she said to Prunella, 'but humans always make things so difficult!'

'Now, Wal,' said Uncle Flea proudly. 'He's always been top dog at looking human. Why, he goes down to town once or twice a month! All dressed properly and in a car and everything.'

'Ah yes,' said Prunella slowly. 'Uncle Wal. I was going to ask about him.'

'Ask away!' Aunty Paws crossed over to the fridge and began to get platters out for lunch. 'Will rat casserole and cornflakes do you pups?' she asked.

Buster saw Prunella's face pale. 'How about a sandwich?' he suggested. 'Er ... peanut butter and beetroot?'

'I hate peanut butter,' admitted Prunella.

'Do you?' Aunty Paws beamed. 'So do I! And there was Wal saying all humans love it! Well, we've got cheese, sliced corgi, lettuce. There's some flies too, though they've slowed down a bit since I caught them yesterday. Must be the chocolate coating.'

'Cheese and lettuce, please,' said Prunella quickly.

'Corgi and tomato, please,' said Buster. 'And a big bowl of milk. But in a glass for Prunella.'

Prunella gulped. 'Thank you.'

Aunty Paws put Buster's sandwich in his bowl by the back door, then passed Prunella's to her on a plate.

'Sure you wouldn't like a nice bone for afters?' she asked. 'I've had them buried for a few weeks. They should taste perfect by now.'

Prunella's face froze. 'No, thank you,' she said politely. 'I'm not all that hungry. This will do me fine!' She looked around the kitchen — at Buster lapping up his milk and Uncle Flea lying in old-dog-with-his-nose-pressed-to-his-bum position and Aunty Paws wrapping up the sliced corgi. 'Look, there's something I really, really have to say. I wouldn't be doing my job as a detective if I didn't!'

'Yes, dear?' Aunty Paws smiled at her brightly. Uncle Flea pricked up his ears.

'It's about Uncle Wal,' said

Prunella slowly. 'And Buster's mum and dad. I mean, it all makes sense.'

Buster looked up from his corgi sandwich. 'What does?'

'Don't you see?' cried Prunella. 'Who had something to gain by your parents' disappearance? Uncle Wal! He's leader of the pack now. Who is the one who hasn't been able to find them, even though he's been in charge? Uncle Wal. Who has a car — the only car on the mountain — that could have carried them away so there'd be no scent trail?'

'Uncle Wal,' said Buster slowly. 'But that's impossible!'

'Your parents wouldn't have got into a car with a stranger,' said Prunella.

'Not in wolf form,' agreed Uncle Flea reluctantly.

'So who would they trust?'

'Uncle Wal. But ... but he'd *never* hurt Mum and Dad!' protested Buster desperately. 'Except in a proper challenge fight,' he added. 'But Uncle Wal would never challenge Dad.'

'The pup's right,' agreed Uncle Flea. 'Wal just isn't strong enough to beat Buster's dad!'

'How do you *know* Uncle Wal wouldn't hurt them?' demanded Prunella.

Buster hesitated. His sixth sense told him Uncle Wal would *always* be loyal to Mum and Dad. But it was hard to explain sixth-sense feelings.

'I just do,' he said lamely.

'I know he's your uncle,' said Prunella more gently. 'But don't you see? It all fits together! Uncle Wal could have offered them a ride, then just driven them away!'

Uncle Flea shook his head. 'But don't you see, girl?' he barked. 'A werewolf can't hide things from another werewolf! I smell Wal's bum every day when he comes home. He doesn't smell guilty.'

'How does he smell then?' asked Prunella.

'He smells of talcum powder,' said Buster quietly. 'Ever since Mum and Dad disappeared, Uncle Wal smells of talcum powder. How can you tell what someone is thinking when all you can smell is talcum powder and aftershave?'

Prunella shook her head. 'Uncle Wal *has* to be the kidnapper — I mean wolfnapper! He must have wanted to be pack leader for years, and wolfnapping Buster's parents was the only way to do it! It's the only thing that makes sense!'

Chapter 11

Searching for Uncle Wal

'I still can't believe it!' said Buster sadly. Uncle Wal had bought him his first squeaky plastic rabbit! And taken him for his first ride in a car and let him chew the seat!

'I reckon we have to follow him!' said Prunella. 'See what he does when he goes off in that car of his!'

'Maybe you're right,' said Buster slowly. He tried to think. If they followed Uncle Wal and all he did was look for Mum and Dad that would show Prunella he wasn't guilty. She'd see that all Uncle Wal was doing was ... Buster hesitated. What *was* Uncle Wal doing down off the mountain every day?

'He'll smell us if we try to follow him,' said Aunty Paws nervously. 'Then he'll snarl and raise his hackles ... you just don't understand what it's like for a wolf when your pack leader is angry with you!' she added.

'And Uncle Wal is mostly angry these days. Don't know what's come over him!' Uncle Flea put in, bending down to lick his ...

'Uncle Flea!' hissed Buster. 'Not in front of Prunella! She doesn't like it!'

'But I'm just licking my ... oh, alright,' said Uncle Flea hurriedly. He shook his head. 'Humans have funny ways sometimes. How are you supposed to clean yourself properly if ...'

'You can wear scent!' said Prunella quickly. 'Lots and lots of scent. No, I don't mean to clean your ... your whats-its! I mean so Uncle Wal doesn't smell you! And he won't recognise my smell anyway. Then if he's acting suspiciously, we can confront him, and demand to know what he did with Buster's parents.'

'He won't have Mum and Dad,' insisted Buster loyally, trying to ignore the niggle in his brain.

'That's right!' barked Uncle Flea.

Prunella shook her head. 'You have to admit Uncle Wal is acting strangely!' she said. 'What's he hiding? You have to find out!'

Uncle Flea scratched his neck with his hind leg. 'Don't know how we'd do that,' he muttered, snapping at the flea he'd disturbed.

'Can't you track his car?' asked Prunella.

'Sure! You can, can't you, Uncle Flea?' cried Buster. 'You're the second-best tracker the pack has ever had! Dad said so!'

'Well, I might be able to, even with all the other cars out there,' admitted Uncle Flea. 'That smell of talcum powder is pretty strong. The biggest thing that worries me is going down to town ...' Uncle Flea whined and put his head on his paws. 'It's been years since I went into town,' he confessed. 'You can't teach an old dog new tricks!'

'Please!' begged Buster. 'Even if it's just a chance that Uncle Wal knows what's happened to Mum and Dad, we have to take it!'

Aunty Paws went over to Uncle Flea and bent down and licked his ear comfortingly. She looked back at Buster and Prunella. 'We'll do it,' she said softly. 'If this is what we have to do, we'll do it.'

Half an hour later, the four of them were headed down the mountain and into town.

Uncle Flea had dug out an old dog cart, and Buster had harnessed him and Aunty Paws into it. He and

Prunella sat in the cart while Uncle Flea and Aunty Paws pulled it down the mountain, with Uncle Flea sniffing the road as they went.

Buster was in human shape now, and properly dressed too. Prunella had inspected his wardrobe, and tactfully suggested the best clothes to wear. She'd even made him put shoes on.

Shoes! thought Buster gloomily, as they bounced down the mountain road. He supposed he'd have to get used to shoes if they all had to move to town. He sighed. It still seemed impossible that Uncle Wal had wolfnapped Mum and Dad! But it was impossible they'd disappeared too. A sudden memory of Uncle Wal letting Buster chew his shoes flashed into his mind. Uncle Wal hadn't even minded that he was still wearing them!

But Prunella was a detective. She knew about things like this! Buster gulped. If Uncle Wal was guilty they had to know.

The dog cart rattled through the forest, then along the narrow road between the paddocks. Aunty Paws held her tail high as she loped along the road, but Uncle Flea's was kept low as he concentrated. Cars slowed down, their drivers staring at them as they

passed. Cows mooed at them, and kids pointed. But Uncle Flea kept his nose to the ground.

Soon they came to the outskirts of town. Uncle Flea halted suddenly at a crossroad, nearly jerking Buster and Prunella out of the dog cart. His nose sniffed this way and that. 'Wal went that way!' Uncle Flea panted. 'That talcum powder stinks,' he added. 'Even a poodle could follow a trail like this!'

The cart lurched into the side street.

'Hold on!' Buster yelled to Prunella.

'I am holding on!' Prunella shouted back. But the cart went more slowly now, as Uncle Flea concentrated among the new scents of the town.

To the right ... now to the left ... now to the right again. Left, right, over a hill and round a bend, left, right, and left again ...

'We'd never have found the way without Uncle Flea's nose,' whispered Buster.

Prunella nodded. Her eyes were shining at the adventure. Buster gulped. It was all part of being a detective to her, he thought. But it was serious for him.

Would they find Mum and Dad? Could Uncle Wal really have wolfnapped them? Buster couldn't help remembering all the times Uncle Wal had played catch with him, tossing the

dried cow pat into the air for him to grab. One of the advantages of human shape was being able to toss a cow pat! And all the times Uncle Wal had brought him home lovely, scrunchy, empty plastic milk bottles to play with ...

The cart clattered on. They had passed right through the town now, keeping to the small roads and suburbs, and were coming out the other side. The houses here had larger gardens and one even had a paddock for a pony.

The road became narrower. The bitumen ended, gravel taking its place. And suddenly there it was, parked under a tree at the side of the road — Uncle Wal's car!

'What's he doing here!' muttered Buster. He looked around. There was nothing to be seen except a cow munching grass on top of the hill, and a few trees rustling in the wind.

The dog cart halted. Buster leapt out and unharnessed Uncle Flea and Aunty Paws, while Prunella ran over to the empty car and peered in the window.

'There's no sign of anyone,' she announced.

Uncle Flea shook the dust off his coat, widdled automatically on the wheels of the cart, then raced over and sniffed around the car.

'He went that way!' he announced, lifting his leg on the left-rear tyre. 'Across the paddock and up the hill! And I smell ...' He sniffed again and frowned. 'Dogs,' he said, 'lots and lots of dogs. And something else. Something strange ...'

Buster sniffed too. Even in human form he could smell it as well. A thick dog scent in the afternoon air, but as well as that, a musty, sweet smell, like, like ...

'Canned dog food!' cried Prunella.

Buster stared at her. 'How do you know? You don't have a wolf's sense of smell!'

'I can smell canned dog food!' stated Prunella. '*Nothing* smells as strong as canned dog food! That's one of the reasons Mum won't have a dog, because dog food stinks so much.'

Buster shook his head. 'Maybe Uncle Wal has called in somewhere to have a snack. Maybe this has nothing to do with Mum and Dad at all.'

'I don't believe it,' snorted Prunella. 'Why would he come all this way just for a snack?'

'Exactly,' said Uncle Flea grimly. 'If Wal was hungry he could just knock over a rubbish bin or something. Much nicer than that dog food stuff. It smells as bad as clean sheets and soap bubbles! Disgusting! No, there's something strange about this. Come on! The scent is coming from over the hill!'

Uncle Flea and Aunty Paws squeezed under the fence and bounded across the tufted grass. Buster

and Prunella ducked through the wires and raced after them.

This was dumb, thought Buster suddenly. Why was he still in human shape? He could go six times as fast on four legs!

Buster shut his eyes, nodded his head twice, then ...

It was like a tummy rumble all through his body, with a nibbling feeling on the way. He could feel his feet growing furrier, his hands getting smaller, and his legs growing shorter but faster too ...

And he was a wolf again.

The grass was closer and the dog food smell almost tasty.

'Come on!' he howled to Prunella. 'And bring my clothes, too!' he added.

'What!' Prunella glared at him. 'Look, buster, you can carry your own blasted clothes!'

Buster ignored her. Prunella sighed, stuffed his clothes into her backpack, then dashed after him.

Chapter 12

The Factory

The building over the hill was two storeys high, with the sort of mirrored windows you couldn't see into. It had a car park and a bitumen road leading up to it, a big sign out the front and giant rubbish bins out the back, that Buster longed to rummage in.

No! he told himself. Concentrate! This is no time to go hunting through rubbish bins!

Uncle Flea and Aunty Paws had stopped, and were loping back to him. 'Wal's smell goes into that building!' Uncle Flea panted. 'And he's Changed!'

'Back into a wolf!' Buster stared. 'Why would he do that?'

'Easier to sneak around as a wolf,' said Uncle Flea.

'Maybe that's why he parked his car over the hill, instead of driving up the main road to the front gate,' said Prunella slowly. 'So he could Change into a wolf without anyone seeing him.'

She narrowed her eyes and read the distant sign. 'Doggie Yums Pet-food Factory and Testing Laboratory,' she read. 'Of course! This is a place where they make dog food! That's why the smell is so strong.'

Buster shook his head. 'But why would Uncle Wal come here?'

'Smells as bad as clean socks,' said Uncle Flea disparagingly. 'Even Wal wouldn't want to eat here!'

'I think I know,' said Prunella grimly. 'If they make dog food here they need dogs to test it on. I bet your dear Uncle Wal sold your parents to be lab dogs!'

Buster sat back in horror. 'What! No! Not Uncle Wal! Uncle Wal wouldn't do that!'

'Not even to be pack leader?' demanded Prunella. 'Not even to try to make the pack turn human, instead of being wolves?'

'No.' Buster wrinkled his nose. Maybe it would make more sense to him if he were in human shape. But now the whole thing seemed dumb! Mum and Dad weren't dogs — they were werewolves. They could Change back to human any time they liked! And if Uncle Wal *had* sold them, why had he come back here as a wolf?

'I just don't understand,' he said aloud.

'Me neither,' panted Aunty Paws.

'Nor me,' barked Uncle Flea.

Prunella nodded. 'Too many mysteries,' she agreed. 'There's only one thing to do.'

'What?' demanded Buster.

Prunella grinned. 'I'll take you three doggies up to the front door, and see if they want to buy you!'

CHAPTER 13

The Trap

The security guard in the sentry box at the front gate was eating a sandwich.

Aunty Paws sniffed. 'Fish paste,' she whispered. 'I love fish paste!'

The guard stared at Buster, Aunty Paws and Uncle Flea. 'They're very big dogs,' he said doubtfully.

'They're Irish wolfhounds,' said Prunella confidently.

The man blinked. 'No they're not!' he objected. 'My brother breeds Irish wolfhounds! Those look more like,' he gulped, 'wolves!'

Prunella forced a laugh. 'Wolves! How would a kid like me get hold of wolves? Of course they're not wolves!'

'Ferocious wolves,' added the guard nervously.

'They're not ferocious at all!' Prunella assured him. 'Act cute,' she hissed out of the corner of her mouth.

Cute! Buster wondered if he should bite her ankle. But this was all for Mum and Dad's sake, he reminded

himself. He could even act cute if it meant saving his parents.

Buster sat on his haunches and launched himself up, his paws in front of his chest. 'Woof, woof,' he said sweetly, letting his tongue hang out in a dribbly doggie grin.

'See?' said Prunella reassuringly. 'The cute doggie woggie is begging! And look, this doggie is playing dead and this one,' she pointed to Uncle Flea, 'just wants to shake hands.'

'What! Oh.' Uncle Flea lifted up one paw. 'Woof, woof, woof,' he growled disgustedly.

The guard gulped. 'That cute little doggie woggie looks like it wants to eat my hand, not shake it! But Miss Snotgrass says we do need more dogs. Half the last batch of dogs we got died of indigestion,' he confessed.

'Who's Miss Snotgrass?' asked Prunella. 'Down,' she hissed to Aunty Paws, who was slobbering at the fish-paste sandwich. 'You're supposed to be playing dead!'

'Miss Snotgrass owns Doggie Yum,' said the guard. He spoke into the two-way radio. 'Miss Snotgrass, it's Jim at the gate,' he said. 'There's a girl here with three dogs she wants to sell. Big dogs. With fangs,' he added.

'All the better,' came the voice from the radio. 'Big dogs eat more! Send her in!'

The barrier lifted. Prunella smiled at the guard, Buster showed his teeth, Aunty Paws grabbed the guard's fish-paste sandwich, Uncle Flea lifted his leg on the corner of the sentry box, and they headed towards the front door.

The door slid open as they approached. There was a lobby with big cushioned chairs, and a reception desk. Behind the desk was a young woman on the phone. She nodded to them as they came in. 'Take a seat,' she said. 'Miss Snotgrass will be with you in a moment.' She went back to her phone call.

Buster leapt up onto one of the seats. Uncle Flea took another.

'Burp!' Aunty Paws vomited up the fish-paste sandwich neatly next to the sofa.

'Sorry,' she whispered, 'I should have remembered fish paste always makes me chuck up. I don't suppose there's any grass in here is there? A few mouthfuls of grass always makes me feel better.'

Prunella edged round the fishy lump so the receptionist wouldn't see it. 'Forget about the grass!' she hissed, and glared at Buster.

'Down, boy!' she ordered. 'Off the chair!'

Buster ignored her.

Prunella cast an embarrassed look at the receptionist. 'Down!' she ordered more loudly.

'Woof,' said Buster coolly.

Prunella bent down. 'Look, buster,' she scowled, 'good dogs don't jump on the furniture! Get off at once!'

'I'm not a dog, I'm a werew—' Buster began, when the door to the laboratory opened, and a woman stepped out.

Miss Snotgrass looked like Mum's age, or a bit older. She had a white coat and a spiky hair cut and she carried a bunch of keys at her waist, and she smelled like . . .

The hackles on Buster's neck rose. She smelled like Mum! And Dad! Buster sniffed again. Miss Snotgrass even smelled of Uncle Wal's talcum powder.

Where were they? There were other smells too. Strange, frightened smells, and not quite meaty smells — smells Buster couldn't understand.

'Woof!' cried Buster urgently, leaping off the sofa. 'Woof, woof!' Beside him Uncle Flea leapt to his feet and howled, and Aunty Flea put her tail between her legs.

Miss Snotgrass blinked. 'A noisy lot,' she said. 'No wonder you want to get rid of them.'

'Er, yes,' said Prunella weakly. 'My mum doesn't like dogs,' she added.

'They're such big ones,' agreed Miss Snotgrass. 'Smelly too.' Prunella edged guiltily around the fish-paste sandwich vomit.

'I can give you fifty dollars each for them. One hundred and fifty dollars altogether. Is that alright?' Miss Snotgrass took a cheque book out of her pocket.

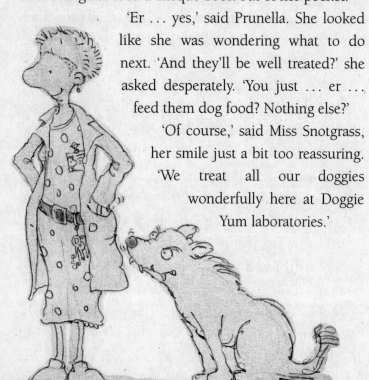

'Er ... yes,' said Prunella. She looked like she was wondering what to do next. 'And they'll be well treated?' she asked desperately. 'You just ... er ... feed them dog food? Nothing else?'

'Of course,' said Miss Snotgrass, her smile just a bit too reassuring. 'We treat all our doggies wonderfully here at Doggie Yum laboratories.'

'That's just wonderful!' Prunella beamed at Miss Snotgrass, but her eyes gleamed as though she had just worked out a plan. What was Prunella up to now? Buster wondered. How were they going to get inside to search for his parents and Uncle Wal?

'You know,' Prunella continued confidentially. 'When I leave school I'd like to be just like you! Wear a white coat and do important work like testing dog food. I don't suppose ...' She looked wistfully up at Miss Snotgrass.

Miss Snotgrass smiled. It looked a more genuine smile this time, thought Buster. 'What?' she inquired.

'I don't suppose I could just *see* your laboratories?' asked Prunella eagerly. 'Only I've never ever seen a real laboratory! It would be *sooo* exciting.'

Miss Snotgrass looked doubtful. 'We don't usually let the public see ...' she began.

'Oh, *please* ...' pleaded Prunella.

Buster looked at her admiringly. If she'd been a dog she would have been sitting up begging!

'Oh, alright,' Miss Snotgrass decided. 'Now, I'll just put these on your dogs.'

SNAP!

'No ...' began Buster. But before he could get the word out, a muzzle had been clipped around his jaws. Even worse, a thick leather collar was latched around his neck. Buster watched mutely as Uncle Flea and Aunty Paws were muzzled too.

How could he speak with a muzzle on?

Even worse, how could he Change back to human with a thick collar on! You had to be able to nod two times to turn human! But this collar didn't let you nod at all!

Was that how Mum and Dad had been captured? he wondered. If they'd had collars on they couldn't turn back into human! And with muzzles they couldn't even talk!

Where were they? Trapped in this horrid concrete box? And how did Uncle Wal fit into this?

It was all up to Prunella now, he realised desperately. Prunella had to save them all!

He glanced at Prunella. Did she understand how desperate things were?

Prunella gave him an almost imperceptible nod.

CHAPTER 14

Cages!

Miss Snotgrass led the way up the corridor, the three dog leads in her hand. 'Now here,' she said proudly, gesturing into a door, 'we have the Doggie Yum trial kitchens!'

Buster peered inside. Great vats with mechanised stirrers were mixing stuff that looked like rabbit guts and peanut butter. But rabbit guts smelled … well … gutsy! thought Buster. This smelled sweet and stale. The sort of stuff you'd only eat if there was nothing else about.

'It looks very, um, impressive,' said Prunella. 'Big!'

'Very big,' Miss Snotgrass said and smirked. 'We can mix

1,000 cans of Doggie Yum in one batch here!' She led the way into the giant room, past the mixing vats, and past a conveyer belt.

Plop! Plop! Plop! A line of nozzles filled each can with gunk, then the conveyer belt passed them into a sealed section. A few metres later the cans emerged, and were labelled with the picture of a grinning, glossy-haired dog.

Ha! thought Buster. If that dog's been eating Doggie Yum, I'm a shih-tzu.

'And that's the end of the process,' said Miss Snotgrass proudly.

'Wow!' breathed Prunella, giving Uncle Flea a nudge as he began to lift his leg on the conveyer belt post. 'And now could we see the doggies? The doggies that test Doggie Yum? Oh, my friends will be so impressed when I tell them I've seen where Doggie Yum is tested! *All* my friends feed their dogs Doggie Yum,' she added, with her fingers crossed behind her back. 'Maybe they could find you more doggies too,' she added innocently.

'Well, alright.' Miss Snotgrass' smile grew even wider at Prunella's flattery. She led the way into another corridor, and then another, down the stairs and along again.

The smell of dogs was stronger now. There was another smell too, Buster realised. The smell of fear, and hopelessness.

Uncle Flea whined. Aunty Paws' tail was between her legs.

Miss Snotgrass opened the door.

Buster stared.

It was a long room, very clean and white. And it was full of cages.

Each cage was just long and wide enough for a dog to stand, or lie down. The cages weren't even big enough for a dog to lift its leg properly, Buster realised in horror.

Each cage held a dog, and a dish of Doggie Yum. Big dogs and small dogs, shaggy dogs and dogs with hair half-fallen out. Dogs with blank, hopeless eyes, wearing collars and muzzles so tight, there was just enough room to put out a tongue to eat their Doggie Yum.

And there, in the middle, were three cages with faces he knew. Mum and Dad. And Uncle Wal!

Uncle Wal hadn't betrayed Mum and Dad, thought Buster. He really had been trying to track them! And he'd been captured too!

The three caged wolves stared out at him. Mum whined in alarm. But the muzzle stopped her from speaking.

'Now you see,' Miss Snotgrass was saying, 'it's all totally hygienic! The cages are cleaned three times a day. This lot of dogs over here are trying a new type of Doggie Yum. It's mostly ground fish bones. Fish bones with meat flavouring are much cheaper than meat. The next lot of dogs are trying a recipe based on old newspapers and urea — that's processed from sewage. It's used a lot in cattle feed. We need to see if the dogs will eat it, and if they get sick, or lose their fur.'

'Oh,' said Prunella. She was staring at the dogs. She seemed too shocked to make even a fake enthusiastic comment. Then suddenly she turned to Miss Snotgrass again. 'It's all been absolutely wonderful!' she said. 'You've no idea what this has meant to me,' she added, and this time her voice sounded totally sincere. 'Do you mind if I just hug my doggies goodbye?'

'Of course, dear,' said Miss Snotgrass. 'And if you ever want a holiday job, you know where to come!'

'Thank you,' said Prunella calmly. She bent down and hugged Uncle Flea, then Aunty Paws, then Buster.

Buster felt Prunella's arms around his neck, and her fingers fiddling with the catch on his collar and muzzle. 'When I say go, Change,' she whispered.

Prunella stood up again. She beamed at Miss Snotgrass. 'I've got a little surprise to say thank you for showing me round!' she said brightly.

Prunella looked at the others to check they were ready. 'Go!' she yelled.

The collars and muzzles fell off Aunty Paws, Uncle Flea and Buster.

'Hurry! Let Mum and Dad and Uncle Wal out!' Buster yelled to Prunella. 'They're the big dogs in the cages at the front!'

Buster shut his eyes, nodded his head twice, then ...

Nunggg!

It was like an earthquake all through his body, with a sort of volcano exploding on the way. He could feel his tongue growing shorter, his feet getting bigger, and his fur disappearing except on his head ...

And he was a boy again.

Suddenly the dogs began to howl! It was a cry of despair at being caged, and terror too. They'd probably never seen dogs turn into humans, thought Buster. And the humans in this place were their tormentors!

Aunty Flea was Changing too. A naked elderly woman with wild hair and fingernails like claws reared up at Miss Snotgrass.

'You ... you monster!' Aunty Paws shrieked.

Miss Snotgrass stared, then screamed. 'No ... no ... werewolves!' she cried. 'Help! Help! Help!'

The caged dogs howled all the louder.

'I'll rip your throat out!' Uncle Flea hadn't bothered to Change. He crouched, his hackles raised, then leapt ...

'No!' yelped Buster. He dashed in front of his uncle and knocked him sideways. 'Don't hurt her!'

'Don't hurt her?!' snarled Uncle Flea, crouching at Buster's feet, his fangs gleaming and drool dripping to the floor. 'Look what she's done! I want to hurt her! I want to . . .'

'No!' yelled Buster again. 'Stop thinking like a wolf, Uncle Flea!'

'I am a wolf!' began Uncle Flea.

Miss Snotgrass was whimpering now. 'Werewolves,' she muttered fearfully. 'Werewolves! *Naked* werewolves,' she mumbled, with a glance down at Buster, and another at the fearsome Aunty Paws. She shrank back as far as she could till her back was to the wall.

'No, you're not a wolf, Uncle Flea!' Buster fumbled for words. 'You're a werewolf! You're human too! Listen to your human half! If you rip her throat out (Miss Snotgrass whimpered again) the police will come and you'll be arrested and everyone will know about us and . . . and who knows what will happen then!'

'He's right,' said a voice.

Buster turned to see who had spoken. It was Uncle Wal. Prunella had got his muzzle off, and Mum's too, and now she was working on Dad's.

'Just what I have been trying to teach you, boy!' barked Uncle Wal approvingly. 'A good werewolf knows when to think like a human!'

'Oh, Buster, darling, I've been so worried about you,' barked Mum, pushing at the door of her cage.

'Me too!' said Uncle Wal gruffly. 'You kept hunting about by yourself. I was afraid the dognappers would get you too, before I tracked them down!'

'Good lad!' Dad bounded out of his cage and sniffed Buster all over to make sure he was alright.

'But we can't just let that woman go on like this!' cried Uncle Flea, sitting back on his haunches. 'Dog-napping, keeping dogs in cages, making them eat Doggie Yum!'

'No!' declared Buster. He turned to Miss Snotgrass. 'Do you know what we are?' he snarled.

'Werewolves!' muttered Miss Snotgrass, cowering in a corner.

'Right,' said Buster. 'And if you ever, ever keep dogs in cages and experiment on them like this again I'm going to the newspapers. I'm going to tell them that Doggie Yum turns dogs into werewolves. I'll tell them I ate Doggie Yum and look what happened to me! I'll tell them that if people buy Doggie Yum one night their dogs will turn into werewolves too and ...'

'Rip their throats out!' put in Uncle Flea with relish. He was drooling again.

'And eat them with chilli sauce and peanut butter,' added Aunty Paws.

Prunella looked at her, shocked.

'Throats taste boring without some sauce,' Aunty Paws explained, with a wink to Prunella and a fierce glance at Miss Snotgrass.

'But that would ruin us!' gasped Miss Snotgrass.

'Exactly,' said Buster.

'But ... but how can we test Doggie Yum without dogs?' whimpered Miss Snotgrass.

Uncle Flea jumped up on his hind legs, his forelegs against Miss Snotgrass' shoulders. '*You* eat it,' he said, with a sharp gust of wolf breath in her face. 'Let's see if it makes *you* sick. And if you can eat it and your hair doesn't fall out, then maybe it's fit to serve to dogs.'

Mum, Dad and Uncle Wal exchanged glances. 'Now!' ordered Dad. The three werewolves shut their eyes, nodded their heads twice, then ...

Nunggg!

'Errrp!' gulped Prunella, staring at Dad and Uncle Wal and then further down at Buster. She quickly shut her eyes. 'Put some clothes on!' she muttered.

She handed Buster the backpack with his clothes in it, still with her eyes shut. Buster handed a shirt to Uncle Wal then began to put his pants on.

'Sorry about that!' Dad's voice was amused. 'Oh, it's so good to stretch again! And it was all my fault,' he added. 'This big van stopped up on the mountain and I just wandered over to lift my leg on its tyres and they grabbed me. Had me muzzled before I knew what was what, and your mum too.' Dad clapped Uncle Wal on the back. 'If I'd just thought like a human for a change they wouldn't have got us!'

'Huh! Being human wasn't enough! When I finally tracked your parents here they grabbed me too,' said Uncle Wal, tying the shirt around him so it covered his bum. 'If it hadn't been for Buster here we'd have had it!'

Dad hugged Buster roughly. 'Congratulations, son! I should have known you'd save us. One day you're going to be the best leader this pack has ever had! And thank you too, Prunella! You can tell her to open her eyes again,' he added. 'I'll Change back.'

'Wouldn't mind Changing too,' remarked Aunty Paws. 'It gets awfully draughty being human.'

Nunggg!

Suddenly Dad and Aunty Paws had fur again.

Mum hugged Buster too, and kissed his cheek. 'You were wonderful!' she said. 'As for you,' she added to Miss Snotgrass. 'If you don't behave yourself, I'm going to make sure you get mange and fleas. Now take your dress off.'

'My … my dress?' whispered Miss Snotgrass.

'Yes,' said Mum.

Miss Snotgrass lifted her dress over her head and stood there in her petticoat, while Mum slipped the dress on over her own head instead. It was a bit short, but not too bad a fit.

'Thank you,' said Mum coolly. 'You can keep the shoes. I'd rather feel the soil under my feet — or paws. Come on, Wallace. Let's get the others out.' She and Uncle Wal began to open all the dog cages.

One by one the frightened dogs slunk out, their tails between their legs.

'Woof! Woooof, woof!' barked Dad.

'That's dog for "You're free now! Widdle on every doorpost you come to and off you go!"' Buster explained to Prunella.

Prunella had her eyes open now. She stared at the scared dogs blinking helplessly at each other. 'But

110

where will they go!' she cried. 'Maybe their owners sold them! Maybe they don't have homes!'

'Good point,' said Mum. 'Some of them were stolen by dognappers, just like we were. We'll have to sniff out where those dogs live and take them home. But others don't have homes. They're strays.' She smiled. 'So they'll just have to come home with us.'

'That's werewolf rule number 11: *Always have enough room for a few dozen more*,' said Dad happily. '*As long as they obey the pack leader*,' he added, showing his teeth a little. 'That's werewolf rule number 12!'

The dogs straightened up at that.

Mum sidled up to Aunty Flea. 'Better get rid of the sliced corgi in the fridge,' she whispered. 'Might scare some of the dogs, and we don't want any nervous messes in the middle of the kitchen floor. Besides, I've lost my taste for corgi. I've really made some good friends here. I never realised that you could be close friends with a dog before.'

'Or a human,' said Buster. He shot a look at Prunella and she blushed. 'Thank you,' he added.

Prunella blushed even harder. 'Thank *you*,' she said. 'You're my first successful case!'

'What happened to the others?' asked Buster.

'There weren't any,' confessed Prunella.

'Come on!' barked Dad. 'Time to be going. Don't widdle yourself, woman,' he added to Miss Snotgrass.

'We'll leave you all safe and sound. As long as you behave yourself!'

Miss Snotgrass nodded, too cowed to say a word. The werewolves strode out, Dad first, his tail held high, followed by Mum, wearing no shoes and Miss Snotgrass' dress, with Aunty Paws trotting beside her. Uncle Wal and Uncle Flea came next, and lastly, Buster and Prunella, and all the dogs behind them, jumping and leaping and enjoying their freedom, and widdling on every doorpost they came to, just as their pack leader had told them to.

The startled workers peered through the doors as the dogs bounded out to freedom.

It was over.

CHAPTER 15

Partners

It was cool up on the Tower roof. The night air was sweet. The moon rose round as an orange and bright as gold.

'Now you stretch your throat right up ...' instructed Buster, 'then hooowwwlll!'

The sound floated down the mountain and over the trees.

'Howl!' Prunella copied him. The sound hiccuped a bit, then grew stronger.

Buster grinned. 'That was pretty good for a human,' he admitted.

'Thanks,' said Prunella, grinning back at him. 'This is fun!'

'Do you *really* think school will be fun, too?' Buster asked. Dad had decided that Uncle Wal was right. The pack *did* need to learn how to cope in a human world. As Uncle Wal had said, if they'd known how to be human they could have gone to the police when Mum and Dad had been abducted.

And the first step for Buster in learning how to be human was to go to school. Prunella had given Mum and Aunty Paws a makeover and was teaching Dad and Uncle Flea and Uncle Wal what a well-dressed werewolf really ought to wear. And in return, they were teaching her how to track, plus the finer points of bum sniffing.

One day, thought Buster, he might even work out how to explain to Prunella how to get a sixth sense.

'Some of school is boring,' Prunella admitted. 'But most of it's okay. And you learn to understand how the world works too.' She glanced at Buster, then quickly glanced away. 'You know, Buster,' she added shyly.

'Know what?' asked Buster, surprised. He'd never known Prunella to sound shy before. Or smell shy either! And he was pretty sure that 'Buster' had a capital letter!

'You and me ... we make a good team. As detectives,

114

I mean — your tracking and my thinking. No matter how much I practise, I'll never be as good at tracking and understanding bum smells as you.'

'I don't think I'll ever be as good at human thinking as you either,' admitted Buster. 'You've had so much more experience!'

'Well,' Prunella looked more embarrassed than ever. 'You don't think you might like to, well, join my detective agency? As a partner?'

Buster grinned. 'There's only one thing to say to that!' he said happily.

'What?' asked Prunella hopefully.

'Hooowwwlll!'

Prunella grinned and joined in.

Other Titles by Jackie French

Wacky Families Series

1. My Dog the Dinosaur • 2. My Mum the Pirate
3. My Dad the Dragon • 4. My Uncle Gus the Garden Gnome
5. My Uncle Wal the Werewolf • 6. My Gran the Gorilla (January 2006)

Phredde Series

1. A Phaery named Phredde • 2. Phredde and a Frog Named Bruce
3. Phredde and the Zombie Librarian • 4. Phredde and the Temple of Gloom
5. Phredde and the Leopard-Skin Librarian
6. Phredde and the Purple Pyramid
7. Phredde and the Vampire Footy Team
8. Phredde and the Runaway Ghost Train (November 2005)

Outlands Trilogy

In the Blood • Blood Moon • Flesh and Blood

Historical

Somewhere Around the Corner • Dancing with Ben Hall
Soldier on the Hill • Daughter of the Regiment
Hitler's Daughter • Lady Dance • The White Ship
How the Finnegans Saved the Ship • Valley of Gold
Tom Appleby, Convict Boy • They Came on Viking Ships

Fiction

Rain Stones • Walking the Boundaries
The Secret Beach • Summerland
Beyond the Boundaries • A Wombat Named Bosco
The Book of Unicorns • The Warrior – The Story of a Wombat
Tajore Arkle • Missing You, Love Sara • Dark Wind Blowing
Ride the Wild Wind: The Golden Pony and Other Stories

Non-fiction

Seasons of Content • How the Aliens From Alpha Centauri Invaded My
Maths Class and Turned Me into a Writer
How to Guzzle Your Garden • The Book of Challenges
Stamp, Stomp, Whomp (and other interesting ways to get rid of pests)
The Fascinating History of Your Lunch
Big Burps, Bare Bums and other Bad-Mannered Blunders
To the Moon and Back • Rocket Your Child into Reading
The Secret World of Wombats (August 2005)

Picture Books

Diary of a Wombat • Pete the Sheep

Jackie French

Jackie French's writing career spans 14 years, 39 wombats, 110 books for kids and adults, 15 languages, various awards, radio shows, newspaper and magazine columns, theories of pest and weed ecology and 28 shredded-back doormats. The doormats are the victims of the wombats, who require constant appeasement in the form of carrots, rolled oats and wombat nuts, which is one of the reasons for her prolific output: it pays the carrot bills.

Jackie's most recent awards include the 2000 Children's Book Council Book of the Year Award for Younger Readers for *Hitler's Daughter*, which also won the 2002 UK Wow! Award for the most inspiring children's book of the year; the 2002 Aurealis Award for Younger Readers for *Café on Callisto*; ACT Book of the Year for *In the Blood*; and for *Diary of a Wombat* with Bruce Whatley, the Children's Book Council Honour Book, NSW Koala Award for Best Picture Book, Nielsen Book Data / ABA Book of the Year Award, the Cuffie Award for favourite picture book (USA) and the American Literary Association (ALA) for notable children's book.

Visit Jackie's website

www.jackiefrench.com

or

www.harpercollins.com.au/jackiefrench
to subscribe to her monthly newsletter

Stephen Michael King

Stephen's first picture book, *The Man Who Loved Boxes*, was nominated for the Crighton award for illustration, was the winner of the inaugural Family Award and was selected for Pick of the List (US). He has since illustrated over 20 books, and has been shortlisted five times for the Children's Book Council Awards. In 2002 he won both the Yabba and Koala children's choice awards for *Pocket Dogs*.

Stephen and his family live on a coastal island in a mud brick house on 10 acres of organic orchards, rainforests and visiting wildlife.

My MUM the PIRATE

Cecil's mum wears long black boots and an even longer sword, and she makes her enemies walk the plank. Putrid Percival serves sea monster soup for dinner, when Cecil would rather eat pizza. Filthy Frederick stinks — but hey, he's good at maths, and nobody's perfect! All Cecil wants is a normal life.

With parent–teacher night looming, Cecil is worried. Will his mum ruin Cecil's newly found street-cred as 'CJ'? But when flood waters strike and Bandicoot Flats Central School is in danger, who will save the students and teachers from the perils of the rising waters? And is Cecil's mum really a pirate?

My Dog the DINOSAUR

Gunk's dad wears fluffy chicken slippers. His sister, Fliss, is into weightlifting and his mum is searching for aliens. Gunk has Spot, his pet dog ... or is it? (A dog, that is.)

Spot has a long neck, a flat tail and eats lettuce. Lots of it. Come to think of it, Spot is the silliest-looking dog Gunk has ever seen. Spot is scared of cats, too, and Fliss's motorbike. And then Spot starts to grow ...

Will Spot ever learn how to bark? What strange secret does Pete, the girl next door, keep in her shed?

Can Gunk teach Spot to like dog food? Or, will everyone in the world want to take Spot away when they find out that he isn't really a dog?

My DAD the Dragon

Horace's dad has silver wings and a green and orange tail. His mum hasn't been able to cast a spell right yet, and his sister Grub — the Fayre Elayne — invents weird things like a box that can take instant pictures.

At King Arthur's School for Knights the nasty Sir Sneazle has given Horace the worst assignment of all. Why couldn't Horace be asked to rescue a damsel in distress instead of Pimply Pol, Bran and Snidge, or write an essay on the broadsword instead of Bernard. Anything but kill a dragon!

How will Horace and his friends manage? Will the Fayre Elayne come to the rescue with one of her inventions? Can Mum cast a spell that really works? And will Horace finally discover the truth about his family that will save Dad and Camelot?

My Uncle Gus the
GARDEN GNOME

Tom has the happiest family around. Dad is Senior
Bogeyman for the entire east coast and Mum is First
Assistant Tooth Fairy. Tom loves being around Fra and his
best friend, Mog, a large and hairy … well, no one is quite
sure what Mog is. And then there's Uncle Gus — everything
seems to be right when Uncle Gus is around.

But Tom soon finds out what happens when you don't take
the daughter of the Most Powerful Witch in the World to the
school dance. Bad luck! A meal of mutant spaghetti, a magic
carpet ride through a sewerage channel, and an unwelcomed
visit from Kitty-Kat the sabre-toothed tiger has turned Tom's
world upside down.

Sometimes it takes a small person to make a big difference.
In this delightful wacky adventure of fun and mayhem
discover how a little garden gnome can put things right.